SPORT OF KINGS

STEPHEN TAYLOR

STEPHEN TAYLOR BOOKS

ISBN: 978-1-7391636-4-8

DANNY PEARSON WILL RETURN

For updates about current and upcoming releases, as well as exclusive promotions, visit the authors website at:

www.stephentaylorbooks.com

ALSO BY STEPHEN TAYLOR

THE DANNY PEARSON THRILLER SERIES

Snipe

Heavy Traffic

The Timekeepers Box

The Book Signing

Vodka Over London Ice

Execution Of Faith

Who Holds The Power

Alive Until I Die

Sport of Kings

Blood Runs Deep

Command to Kill

No Upper Limit

Leave Nothing To Chance

CHAPTER 1

Danny stretched back on the sofa trying his best to stifle the Chinese takeaway and lager belch building in his stomach. It didn't work, and a deep burp emanated from his mouth.

'Oi. It didn't take living together long before the standards started to slip, did it? You'll be walking around farting next,' said Alice looking up from her snuggled position with a smirk on her face.

'Sorry, dear,' Danny replied sarcastically.

He looked down into her striking emerald green eyes and bent forward, kissing her passionately on the lips.

'You're forgiven,' she said when they parted.

'Shall we go up?'

'Ok, I'll just clear this lot up first,' said Alice yawning as she got up off the sofa.

'I'll do it, you go up. I'll be there in a minute,' Danny replied getting up and rubbing his full belly.

'Hmm,' Alice said, eyeing his stomach.

'What?'

'It's ok, honey, I like the dad bod look,' she said teasing him.

'You cheeky bugger,' Danny said sucking it in and puffing out his chest. 'I'm in the best shape ever.'

'Ok, Rambo, if you say so,' Alice said, laughing as she climbed the stairs.

Danny looked down and patted his belly.

Big Dave's gym for you tomorrow, mate.

He'd loaded the dishwasher, put the rubbish out and was on his way upstairs when his phone rang.

'Hello.'

'Danny, it's Smudge. I'm in trouble, mate. I need your help.'

'What's up?' said Danny, turning serious at Smudge's tone.

'I fucked up, mate. Shit. I got involved with some heavyweights, nasty bastards. I didn't like what they were doing, so I told them I was out. The fuckers tried to kill me. I got away by the skin of my teeth. Totalled my car on the way out,' said Smudge opening the curtains a crack to take a nervous peep outside.

'Can't you go to the police?' said Danny, already knowing Smudge wouldn't.

'No, they own the police. I'm fucked, mate, you've got to help me.'

'Ok, ok, calm down, Smudge. Where are you?' Danny said, already sliding on his trainers and grabbing his coat.

'I'm at my Nan's old holiday chalet in Sea Palling, Norfolk. You remember where it is, you came up here with me and Fergus and went sea fishing,' said Smudge, talking fast with nerves.

'Alright, sit tight. I'm on my way,' said Danny hanging up.

Smudge tucked his phone in his jacket and took another peep out the window, before moving upstairs to the main bedroom of the small timber-framed holiday chalet. He grabbed a large canvas bag and emptied it out on the floor, along with his drysuit, regulator and other diving gear. Something wrapped in a towel thudded to the ground. Smudge picked it up and unwrapped it on the bed. The sound of approaching cars tore his eyes away from the plastic-sealed brick of white powder. He flicked the light switch and scooted over in the darkness to the window.

'Shit, shit, shit,' he said through gritted teeth, the sight of the two black Nissan pickup trucks putting fear into his heart. Smudge turned and grabbed the brick off the bed. Looking around in a panic, he opened the airing cupboard and shoved it behind the hot water tank. With the sound of the vehicles pulling to a halt out front, Smudge threw open the rear window and hopped out onto the flat roof above the kitchen. Without looking back, he ran to the edge and leaped off into the soft dunes behind the chalet. Fighting against the sand, Smudge started to get traction and passed the summit, half-running, half-stumbling his way down onto the sandy beach on the other side. Heading for the lights of Sea Palling in the distance and the concrete ramp used to get boats and jet skis onto the beach, Smudge dug deep, his lungs burning as he continued to run flat out in the loose sand.

Just got to get to the pub and people. They can't touch me there.

Risking a look behind him, Smudge's heart sank at the sight of two shadowy figures charging up the beach after him. Tucking his head down, he took advantage of the adrenaline surging through his body and ran faster towards the moonlit ramp only a few hundred metres ahead.

Fuck 'em, fuck the lot of them. I'm out of here.

All thoughts of outrunning them came crashing down when one of the Nissan pickup trucks came hurtling down the slope ahead of him, sliding sideways in a cloud of flying sand as it headed towards him. Without breaking momentum, Smudge headed for the dunes. Climbing the slope as the truck slid to a stop behind him, the grunts and breathing of the two men chasing him grew louder every second. He reached the summit and grasped at a glimmer of hope as the lights of the pub blazed into view. The panoramic view disappeared in a flash as a shadow loomed up in front of him. An enormous crack to the side of his head put him into darkness.

'Get him in the truck,' the shadowy figure said to the other two as they wheezed and coughed from the chase.

'Fuck, hang on a minute, Slade. I've—just—got—to get my—breath back.'

Recovering, they picked Smudge up by the feet and arms and carried him back down the slope. Digging some gaffer tape out of the pickup, they taped Smudge's hands and feet before throwing him in the back. Slamming the door shut, Slade caught sight of two heads staring at them from above the dunes. The young couple's faces were pale in the moonlight, with looks of shock and fear on them at what they'd just witnessed.

'Get them,' Slade snarled.

The three of them spread out and moved in. The young couple stood in a panic, bringing the woman's pregnant belly into focus.

'Stay back, I'm calling the police,' said the man, frantically trying to get his phone out of his pocket.

Slade caught up to him as he got the phone free. Grabbing his wrist, Slade headbutted him to the floor unconscious. His girlfriend started to scream, but one of the other men put his hand over her mouth and grabbed her. Reaching into his pocket, Slade pulled the roll of gaffer tape out and peeled a strip back as the terrified woman's eyes went wide and she shook in fear.

CHAPTER 2

Danny walked into the bedroom just as Alice came out of the en-suite bathroom, a puzzled look on her face at Danny with his trainers and jacket on.

'Sorry, love, I've just had a call from an old Regiment friend. He's in trouble, I've got to go,' said Danny, torn between wanting to stay and having to help his old brother in arms.

Alice could see the pained look on his face. She walked up to him and put her hands on either side of his face and pulled him in to kiss him.

'Go on. Go and help your friend.'

Danny pulled back and smiled at her. 'I'll call you in the morning.'

He grabbed his keys and wallet on the way out, calling a number as he headed for the car.

'Fergus, it's Danny. Yeah, sorry it's late. It's Smudge, he's in trouble.'

'Where is he?'

'Up at his Nan's old place on the coast. Norfolk,' said Danny, glad to hear his old SAS buddy's voice.

'Have you called Chaz?' said Fergus, rustling about as he got dressed.

'Not yet, I'm coming to yours now,' said Danny starting up his BMW M4 with a throaty rumble.

'Ok, I'll call him. I'll see you in a bit,' said Fergus in operation mode, hanging up to call Chaz straight away.

Driving as fast as he dared through London's urban jungle, Danny pulled up outside Fergus's tiny terrace house in Enfield. He gave the horn a quick tap and waited. The front door opened, letting the sound of arguing out along with Fergus.

'That's right, your mates call and you go running. Go on, sod off then. I'm better off without you,' shouted Fergus's wife, slamming the front door furiously behind him.

'Good to see you, mate, now put your foot down before she changes her mind and comes after me,' said Fergus, grinning at Danny.

'I see Carol's mellowed,' said Danny, chuckling as he pulled away.

'Yeah, right. If we get there and Smudge is sitting watching TV with a beer in his hand, I'm going to kill him myself.'

'I know he's an idiot, but he sounded scared, Ferg. He said they were trying to kill him, and he meant it. Did you get hold of Chaz?' said Danny, turning serious.

'No, Gaynor said he's on a demolition job in Scotland, she's going to get him to call us.'

'Good, let's get up there,' Danny said, pushing them into their seats as he dropped a gear and accelerated away.

'So what did Smudge say exactly?'

'Not much really. He said he'd got involved with some heavyweights and when he tried to back out, they tried to kill him. Oh, and when I mentioned the police, he said they own the police. That's it,' Danny replied, taking the slip road to join the M11 towards Cambridge.

When Fergus didn't answer, Danny took a sideways glance and saw Fergus looking at him like an excited schoolboy with a big grin on his face.

'What the fuck's the matter with you?'

'I've been working my arse off seven days a week delivering parcels for fucking Amazon. I was getting to the point where I'd sell my soul for a bit of action. I'm getting that buzz, mate,' said Fergus, still grinning.

'Alright, Rambo, keep a lid on it. We all miss the Regiment, Ferg,' said Danny, going from jokey to a serious sadness.

The atmosphere went sombre in the car as they both sat thinking about their SAS days. After an awkward couple of minutes, Danny broke the silence. 'Right, that's enough moping about, we'll sort that dipstick Smudge out, meet up with Chaz when he's back, and drink until we puke and pass out.'

'Thanks, brother,' said Fergus, glad to be back with his friend and old team leader.

CHAPTER 3

A fuzzy confusion, followed by nausea, followed by pain, hit Smudge in shattering waves as he came round. He tentatively opened his eyes, closing them instantly when the harsh electric strip lights set off sparks in his splitting head. He took a few breaths to clear the nausea, then opened his eyes again, millimetre by millimetre. When they'd adjusted enough to focus, all that greeted him was a smooth grey concrete wall. Moving his eyes down told him he was lying on a blue, plastic covered mattress. Smudge remained motionless, breathing slowly as he waited for the pain in his head to move within limits he could handle. When it did, he rolled over slowly, the skin on the side of his face pulling as the sticky dried blood tried to hold him to the mattress.

The room was a smooth concrete cube with a bed, stainless steel fixed toilet and stainless steel sink. Harsh strip lights adorned the ceiling, covered with anti-tamper mesh cages. The bed he lay on was just a mattress on top of a concrete platform. Looking down towards his feet, he saw a solid metal door with trap doors top and bottom and a large, mirrored window to the left-hand side.

Throwing his legs over the side of the bed, Smudge made the mistake of standing up. His head exploded in pain, the concussion putting him back down on his arse. Several minutes later the pain subsided, and Smudge tried again, slowly this time. He shuffled over to the mirrored window and tentatively touched the blood-caked, egg-sized lump on his head while checking his reflection in the window.

Well, this fucking sucks, but on the plus side I ain't dead yet, which means they want me alive for something. Hang in there, Smudge, Danny Pearson's coming.

Backing away from the mirror, Smudge stared into it with a defiant *fuck you* look. He eventually turned and walked to the sink. Cupping his hands, he washed the dried blood off his face and dabbed the lump on his head. When he'd finished, he lay back on the bed and followed his training from the SAS days. Conserve your energy and keep your mind strong, because when the opportunity arises, you've got to be ready to take it.

'Yeah, keep staring, tough guy, it won't help you now. You should have taken the money and kept your mouth shut,' Barney muttered to himself from the observation room behind Smudge's cell.

'Compared to this shit, drug smuggling's fucking nursery school shit,' Barney continued to mutter as he left the room. He wandered across the large concrete space that centred ten cells, each with its own observation room.

Barney Stock lived up to his name. He was short and

stocky with no neck and forearms like Popeye. At first glance, he looked like the missing link.

'Let's see how our other guests are doing,' he said entering an observation room. 'Hello, darlin'.'

Barney moved close to the glass. A dangerous twinkle filled his eyes as he stared at the young pregnant woman curled up in the fetal position, sobbing uncontrollably. With his breath steaming a circle on the one-way glass, Barney turned sideways to look out the door. With no one around, he pushed the door to the observation room closed and returned to the glass. Standing motionless, Barney got off on her fear. Getting increasingly excited at her despair, he moved his hand down and unzipped his flies.

'Barney, where the fuck are you?' came a shout from outside.

'You'll keep,' muttered Barney, zipping himself back up again. He pulled open the door and strolled out. 'I'm here, what do you want?'

'Slade wants you upstairs. He's got some fresh meat. A right lively fucker.'

'Ok, ok, I'm coming, Des. We'll put him in number five,' said Barney, punching the green button before following Des up the stairs.

The Portakabin office in the corner of the giant hay barn slid back to reveal the concrete stairs. Des and Barney walked up into the large space in front of the stored hay bales. Parked inside the barn with its back doors facing them was a battered white Transit van. Vincent Slade grappled with a large man in the back as he fought and kicked out, trying to free himself from his tied hands and feet, unable to see with a cloth sack secured over his head.

'About fucking time,' Slade said to the pair.

Barney wandered up to the back of the van, a passive unimpressed look on his face. Without warning, he powered a punch into the man's stomach with his gorilla-like arm. The guy doubled up, coughing and wheezing, trying desperately to get air into his winded lungs. Standing back, Barney pulled a flick knife out of his pocket and popped the blade up. He cut the rope tying the man's legs with one movement of the razor-sharp blade.

'Grab that side, Des,' said Barney, waiting a second before the two of them pulled the wheezing guy out into the barn. Grabbing an arm each they led him down the steps.

'Tuck him in, Barney, I'll be back in the morning,' said Slade, slamming the van doors before jumping in the driving seat. He watched the Portakabin slide back over the steps until all that could be seen was the Portakabin with the floor-to-ceiling stack of hay bales behind it. Slade drove back out into the darkness, turning back along the two-mile-long dirt track that led to the coast road, six miles away from Sea Palling.

CHAPTER 4

Tired and weary after a breakneck drive, Danny rumbled the powerful car into Sea Palling. Everything was dark and quiet in the early hours. Driving from memory, Danny turned at the pub and chip shop. He followed the narrow road until it wound round to run parallel with the sand dunes and a row of holiday homes. Some of them were no more than glorified sheds with overgrown gardens; some were shiny and new and expensive with statement landscaped gardens.

'Which one is it?' said Fergus squinting out into the darkness.

'It's here somewhere. It's been a few years, but I'll know it when I see it,' said Danny, lowering the window for a better view.

'Hang on, that's it, I remember the blue door,' said Fergus, pointing to the small chalet style shack ahead.

Danny pulled onto the two strips of gravel, with long grass growing in the middle that served as a drive. They got out and walked to the front door to find it slightly ajar. Instinctively the two peeled off to either side of the door.

Danny reached forward and gently pushed it open with the back of his hand. He took a quick look into the small shadowy kitchen, his brain still processing the image as he pulled back out beside the door. The place was dark and quiet, and he didn't get the sense anyone was inside. Signalling to Fergus to peel left into the lounge when they entered, Danny rushed in to the right to check the kitchen. Without having to look, he knew Fergus had passed him into the lounge. The two stood motionless in the dark, listening.

When they heard a banging sound upstairs, they both looked at each other. Danny reached over and slid a carving knife out of its block on the kitchen worktop. Fergus moved to the log burner and pulled a metal poker out of the log basket. The two of them closed up together by the stairs and climbed — almost floated — up to the source of the noise. When they neared the top, Danny could tell it was a rhythmic sound of something slamming in the wind. Relaxing, he walked into the bedroom and flicked on the light. The bedroom window banged lightly in the breeze. Danny stepped over Smudge's clothes and diving gear littered around the floor to close it.

'I know Smudge is a messy bastard, but this is a bit much,' said Fergus from behind Danny.

'Looks like he left in a hurry,' said Danny, moving to one side to let Fergus see out the window.

The two of them looked down at the footprints in the moss on the flat roof below. They followed the scuffing marks leading to the far end where Smudge had run and leaped into the dunes.

'I'll go check around out back,' said Fergus, flicking on the landing light before disappearing downstairs.

Danny looked at Smudge's dive bag sitting on the bed

half packed, and then at the turfed out drysuit, BCD vest, regulators and mask on the floor.

What have you got yourself into, Smudge?

Moving around the room, Danny checking out the wardrobes and drawers, finding nothing other than odd bits of Smudge's clothes. He opened the airing cupboard door and closed it again at the sight of the hot water tank. Something in his subconscious stopped him. He opened it again, trying to figure out what was niggling him. The top of the tank was thick with dust apart from four fresh marks where someone had dragged their fingers across it. Curious, Danny felt around the back of the tank, his finger touching something solid wedged behind it. Working it free, he pulled a plastic-sealed brick of white powder out. Frowning as he backed up, Danny spun the brick over in his hand.

'There are fresh footprints leading up the dunes to the beach. Three sets. One starting part way up where someone jumped off the roof, and two more leading from the side of the house up after him,' came Fergus's voice as he came back up the stairs.

'I think I've got a fair idea what Smudge got mixed up in,' said Danny, waving the brick at Fergus as he came in the room.

'Fuck me, look at the bloody size of it. That stupid bastard,' said Fergus, surprised.

'Yeah well, Smudge always did have a habit of making shit decisions.'

'What do we do now?' said Fergus.

Danny looked at the 3:00 a.m. displayed on his trusty old G-Shock watch.

'Well, I'm going to sleep, mate. I'll flip you. Heads I get the bed, tails I take the sofa,' Danny said with a grin, digging out a coin from his pocket.

'Go on then,' Fergus said, yawning.

Danny flicked the coin in the air, caught it and slapped it on the back of his hand.

'For fuck's sake, every bloody time,' Fergus said as Danny uncovered the coin with the Queen's head facing up.

'Get some sleep, Ferg, we'll figure out what to do next in the morning.'

Danny placed the brick on the side and cleared Smudge's stuff from the bed. He stripped out of his clothes, clicked the light off and got in bed. Still true to his days in the SAS, where you learn to sleep any time, any place, he was asleep within a few minutes.

CHAPTER 5

Lord Bartholomew Harrington-Smythe sat in the drawing room of his ancestral estate, Lessingham Hall. His butler, Timms, entered the room carrying His Lordship's tea and newspapers, as he did every morning at 7:30 a.m. sharp.

'Thank you, Timms. I believe that's Chief Constable Metcalf's car approaching. Be a good fellow and show him in,' Barty said eyeing the blue Volvo working its way up the mile-long drive to the hall.

'Yes sir,' Timms said, turning smartly to leave the room.

I wonder what Metcalf will be whining about today.

After pouring his tea, Barty sat back in his chair and opened the large Guardian newspaper in front of him. As intended, it totally obscured anyone's view of him, setting the stage for Metcalf to have to wait for the Lord's attention. Bang on cue, Timms entered the room with Metcalf in his wake.

'Chief Constable Metcalf to see you, sir,' said Timms, stepping to one side to wait patiently.

Leaving just enough time to make Metcalf uncomfortable, Barty lowered the newspaper and invited Metcalf to sit in the chair opposite with a wave of his hand.

'Good morning, Peter. Tea, coffee?' he said pleasantly.

'Er, tea please,' Metcalf said taking a seat, careful not to crease his uniform.

Timms gave a curt nod to Barty before leaving the room to prepare more tea. He shut the doors to give them privacy on his way out.

'To what do I owe the pleasure of your company, Peter?' said Barty, deliberately sipping slowly from his china cup.

Metcalf moved uncomfortably in his seat before answering.

'A young couple holidaying with their parents at a caravan park in Sea Palling went missing after a late walk on the beach last night.'

'Mmm, how distressing. The beach can be a dangerous place at night,' said Barty, pausing the conversation as Timms came in with Metcalf's drink. They waited until he left and the doors closed again before continuing.

'Cut the crap, Barty. Slade's men were seen driving like lunatics through the village, then two people go missing. This is going to attract way too much attention. The girl's father is a lawyer for Christ's sake,' said Metcalf, shifting nervously in his seat.

A flash of anger crossed Barty's face. He fixed Metcalf with an unwavering stare. His nostrils flared slightly, giving away his annoyance at being spoken to so rudely. The moment only lasted a few seconds before Barty's composure returned and he leaned in towards Metcalf.

'We had some trouble with one of the men. The couple just happened to get in the way. Bad timing on their part, I'm afraid. Slade has taken care of it. The young man will be found washed ashore. The coroner will assume the couple got into trouble and drowned.'

'What about the girl? There'll be a search and press and TV crews crawling all over the place,' said Metcalf, almost in a panic.

'Show some backbone and deal with it, Peter. When they don't find the woman, it will all blow over, a tragedy, lost to the sea and all that. There's plenty of time before the next event,' said Barty, sitting back and returning to his tea from the bone china cup.

'What is she like?' said Metcalf, his body language changing as he leaned forward slightly. His stare intensified as he looked unblinking at Barty.

'Blonde, young, rather pretty, just your type. And Peter, she's pregnant,' said Barty slowly, deliberately adding the pregnant remark to excite Metcalf, who licked his lips as Barty finished the sentence.

'It will take a lot of effort to make this go away, Barty.'

'And my appreciation will reflect that, Peter. A pregnant girl will make top money in the next event. If you make this go away and make sure no one interferes with our business, she's yours. And the chamber will be at your disposal,' said Barty, placing his cup and saucer on the silver tray.

'I'll take care of it. When can I have her?' said Metcalf, so perversely excited he was almost drooling.

'Patience, Peter, patience. Take care of business first and you can have her on the night of the next event.'

'What about the others?'

'They're nobodies, loners and migrant workers, no one local, and no one's looking for them. Now, if you don't mind, Peter, I have a very busy morning,' Barty said standing, which signalled the conversation was over.

'Sorry, of course, Barty, I'll leave you to it,' said

Metcalf, pulling himself together, straightening his uniform as he shook Barty's hand. With impeccable timing, Timms magically appeared behind them to show Metcalf out.

As he headed off down the long treelined drive, Barty stood at the drawing room window watching him leave. His train of thought was only broken when Timms entered holding the phone.

'Mr Slade for you, sir.'

'Thank you, Timms,' said Barty, taking the phone off him and waiting while he discreetly exited the room, closing the oak panelled doors behind him.

'Good morning, Vincent, is everything on track after your eventful night?' Barty said politely but with no discernible emotion.

'Yes sir, the crew's getting the boat ready for the pickup. We'll drop the package off on the way out to the dive site, about half a mile out. The incoming tide should bring it ashore later this afternoon.'

'Excellent. Get someone to plant some of the girls' clothes on the beach. Metcalf's going to help push it as a tragic accident.'

'Yes sir,' was all Slade said in response.

Hanging up, Barty looked at his watch, 8:30 a.m.

Time to get changed. Tee off at the Royal Norwich Golf Club at 10. It wouldn't do to keep Richard and Sir John waiting.

CHAPTER 6

The sun streaming in through the gap in the curtains woke Danny. Rolling over, he blinked to focus at his trusty old G-Shock watch. 7:34 looked back at him. He rolled out of bed and pulled on his jeans and T-shirt. When the socks and trainers were on, he stood at the window running his fingers through his unruly dark hair, trying to flatten the bedhead tufts of hair back down. His eyes focused on Smudge's footprints in the moss on the kitchen's flat roof. He followed them with his eyes to the far edge, spotting the deep sandy holes where Smudge had landed in the dunes and legged it to the beach. Turning away, Danny focused his attention to Smudge's diving gear. A thick canvas dive bag lay on the floor with his dive gear strewn around it. He picked up a towel from the pile, feeling the dampness in its middle as he brought it to his nose and sniffed it.

Sea water. Still wet from a recent dive.

His eyes landed on the plastic-wrapped powder brick on the bedside table. Danny picked it up and sniffed it, frowning as he touched his tongue onto it.

Salty. What have you got yourself mixed up in, Smudge?

He considered slitting the parcel and tasting the contents like they do in the movies, but he had no idea what heroin or cocaine actually looked or tasted like, so thought better of it. Taking into consideration what he suspected the package to contain, he opened the airing cupboard door and wedged the brick back behind the hot water tank. Leaving the room, Danny could hear Fergus rattling around in the tiny kitchen as he descended the narrow staircase.

'Morning, honey! You made my breakfast yet?' Danny joked.

'You'll be lucky, I can't find enough ingredients to make a coffee, let alone a breakfast,' replied Fergus pulling his head out of a cupboard to throw a grin back at Danny.

'Bollocks to it, there's got to be a café in the village. We can sniff around and see if anyone's seen Smudge at the same time,' said Danny noticing Smudge's house keys in a dish on the windowsill.

The two of them left the car and climbed the dunes behind the chalet. They moved down the other side onto the beach and followed the three sets of footprints heading towards the beach access ramp in the distance.

'You see the tyre prints?' said Fergus as they got nearer to the ramp.

'Yep, bastards cut him off,' said Danny turning to follow the footprints that headed up the dunes.

They stood at the top looking across at the pub on the other side close to the ramp, and the shops and chippy and café-cum-amusement arcade beyond it.

'Do you think he got away?' Fergus finally said.

'Nope.'

'Me neither.'

'Excuse me, gentlemen, can I just ask you a couple of questions?' came a shout from the beach behind them.

Danny and Fergus turned in surprise to see two police officers looking up at them.

'Good morning, officers, how can we help you?' said Danny making his way down to them, a polite smile on his face.

'We're just asking everyone if they've seen this man and woman. They went for a late night stroll on the beach last night and never returned,' the officer said showing them a photocopied picture of the couple with a Crimestoppers number underneath.

'Sorry, we've only just arrived. If I see anything, I'll be sure to let you know,' Danny said, taking the picture off the man.

'Thank you, sir. Have a good day,' the officer said before heading off towards some dog walkers.

'That's gotta be too much of a coincidence,' said Fergus, watching them leave.

'Yep, come on, let's get some breakfast, I'm starving,' Danny said, heading towards the ramp.

Walking down the other side into the village, they could see the Reefs Bar pub on their right and the chip shop behind it, on the road they'd driven in on last night. On the left-hand side of the road was a snack bar and amusement all-in-one. With the lack of other options and the smell of bacon wafting out the door, Danny made a beeline for the entrance. They ordered two large breakfasts with mugs of coffee and took a seat by the window, looking out onto a large car park outside the chippy and shops across the road. As they ate, they watched a group of divers with a twenty-foot rigid inflatable boat or RIB as most people called it, manoeuvring it on its trailer into the car park.

The group was a mix of older couples and younger

individuals. The older couples looked in charge as they loaded cylinders and dive bags onto the RIB. They were obviously a dive club going out for the day. As Danny ordered more toast and coffee, another RIB arrived. They went through the same motions as with the others, similar boat, similar crew. They chatted across to each other, obviously looking forward to the dive. An old tractor chugged its way around the corner, reversed up and hitched the first trailer on. As the tractor towed the RIB past their window, Danny and Fergus watched it chug up the ramp while the divers followed it in their assorted Neoprene wetsuits and nylon layered drysuits.

Danny was contemplating their next move when two brand new black Nissan pickup trucks with blacked-out windows pulled into the car park. They parked up and remained there, engines running, nobody getting out. A couple of minutes later a big Mercedes GLE 4x4 pulled into view towing a large thirty-foot RIB with two huge outboard motors on the back. After reversing it into the car park the driver got out and unhitched the trailer. He instantly caught Danny and Fergus's attention as he looked around checking the area before giving a nod to the pick-ups, who immediately switched off the engines and exited the vehicles.

'What do you say, Ferg? That look like a good place to start our search for Smudge?'

'I reckon so,' Fergus replied, watching the crew of six moving around like a well-rehearsed unit as they loaded up the RIB with nothing but the best dive kit.

'Let's go rattle the cage,' said Danny draining the last of his coffee.

'Absolutely,' said Fergus, following Danny out the door.

CHAPTER 7

'Come on, Dickie, shake a leg,' shouted Lord Bartholomew to a short, overweight man, his cheeks red as he hurriedly pulled his golf trolley to the tee off point for the first hole.

'Steady on, old man, you'll give yourself a heart attack,' said Sir John Riddlesworth as he slid his tee in the soft earth and neatly balanced his golf ball on top.

'Sorry, chaps, got stuck behind some bloody tourists doing ten miles an hour. Bloody riff raff. Bad car, bad driving and an ugly wife, one should be allowed to shoot them on sight,' said Richard Cain in between big gulps of air.

'Well, perhaps we can find them for the next Sport of Kings event, Dickie. You could express your displeasure to them personally,' said Barty, with a smile on his face.

'I say, what a wonderful idea, old man. Do you think we could?' said Richard, grinning as he took a 2-wood out of the bag. He huffed and puffed as he did a couple of practice swings past his ample belly.

Sir John moved to one side after a perfect swing that put his ball just short of the green on the par-3 hole.

'It looks like those lessons are finally paying off, John,' said Barty, pushing his ball and tee into the ground after admiring the shot.

'I should bloody well hope so, the amount the club's golf pro charges for coaching,' said Sir John dryly.

The three of them laughed overly loudly before Barty took his swing and sent his golf ball sailing off after Sir John's.

'Has my missing package turned up yet, Barty? I heard there was some trouble last night. Nothing I should be worried about I hope?' said Sir John, his beady eyes staring intently and his thin-lipped mouth turning down in concern.

'No, no, no, nothing to concern yourself with, John. Slade will find your package, and our pet police chief is taking care of the missing couple,' said Barty, dismissing the comment.

'Splendid, because my associates and their extensive bank accounts are eagerly awaiting the big day,' said Sir John, his mouth flicking up at the corners to display a brief smile.

'Patience, John, we have already fulfilled most of their hunt requests. Slade has located the remaining orders, so everything is on schedule for the big day,' said Barty, maintaining a supreme air of confidence.

'And my request?' said Sir John, turning to look at him.

Barty gave him a smug look. 'I've gone above and beyond, John. I've got one of the elite: an ex-SAS soldier no less.'

Sir John's eyes twinkled, the anticipation of the ultimate hunt burning away inside him.

'Don't forget about me, Barty old man,' said Richard, slicing his ball to the left and groaning as it disappeared into the trees.

'How could I ever forget about you, Dickie?' said Barty marching off down the fairway with his golf trolley.

CHAPTER 8

Danny and Fergus walked across the road and headed across the car park towards the RIB. At over six-feet tall, confident, fit and the look of ex-servicemen, both Danny and Fergus caught the attention of Slade and his crew as they approached.

'Nice boat, I bet she can shift when you open those bad boys up,' said Danny, pointing to the big outboard motors.

Taken by surprise at Danny's jovial exchange of conversation, Slade stood up in the boat, his face serious as he contemplated his response.

'Thanks, yeah, she can move when she wants to,' was all he said, trying to cut the conversation dead.

Danny was having none of it and pushed the conversation further. He walked down the side of the RIB, making it obvious he was checking out their kit as he went.

'Wow, all using rebreathers. That's serious kit for leisure diving. You guys commercial divers?' Danny said, noticing two of the crew looking nervous as they moved in front of a mound of kit stowed under a large plastic tarpaulin.

'Yeah, we're commercial divers. Now if you don't

mind, pal, we've got to get out before the tide turns,' said Slade moving between Danny and the tarpaulin to block the view.

Danny's face hardened and his eyes narrowed as he stared intently at Slade. Fergus did the same, moving up close to Danny.

'I've got a mate who's a commercial diver. He's been diving up here as it goes. Darren Smith, everyone calls him Smudge. We came up here to meet him, but he's disappeared. I don't suppose you know him?' said Danny, his tone telling Slade rather than asking him.

Taking in the others in his peripheral vision, Danny noticed two of the men looking up and shifting around uncomfortably at the mention of Smudge.

'Never heard of him. Now, if you don't mind,' replied Slade growling menacingly, his crew moving closer to intimidate them.

Danny and Fergus continued to stare at Slade, letting the tension build before Danny finally spoke.

'Nice talking to you. Have a great dive,' he said, overly cheerful, before walking away slowly, Fergus by his side.

'What do you reckon, Ferg?'

'They knew who he was. Did you clock the two guarding that tarpaulin? They nearly shit themselves when you mentioned Smudge,' said Fergus, strolling along beside Danny.

'Yep, I'd love to know what they were hiding under it,' Danny said watching the tractor returning from the beach after launching the dive club's boat into the sea.

'Let's grab another cuppa. I fancy a chat with that tractor driver once he's finished launching the bunch of fun sponges back there.'

Grabbing another drink, they took the seat back in the window. Minutes later the tractor towing Slade's RIB chugged past with Slade and his crew following on foot behind it. Danny raised his mug in salute and nodded to Slade with a big smile as he glared in through the window on their way past.

'I think you can stop now, Dan, you've definitely got their attention,' Fergus said with a chuckle.

'Doesn't hurt to make sure, Ferg,' replied Danny, smiling.

The tractor driver reversed the trailer into the sea until the water covered its wheels. Lowering the outboards into the waves, Slade released the RIB from the trailer and put the gurgling engines into reverse. He waved the tractor driver off and turned the boat to face seaward. With his mood as dark as the sea, he threw the throttle forward, lifting the front of the boat up as the outboard engines screamed as the boat bounced over the breakers on its way out to sea.

'Take the wheel, Des, I've got to make a call,' he said, handing over and sitting at the front of the boat to make a call.

'Vincent, this had better be important. I'm just about to tee off the ninth hole,' said Barty, annoyed at the intrusion.

'Two of Smith's buddies have turned up asking lots of questions around the village,' said Slade, shouting over the engine noise.

'So? They can't know anything.'

'They don't look like the type who give up easily.'

'Ok, I'll get Metcalf to send them on their way. And the other matter?' said Barty, pressing the phone hard against his ear to hear Slade.

'We're dealing with that now, sir.'

'Very good, I'll catch up with you this evening.'

Barty had already hung up before Slade could answer. He slid the phone in his kit bag and checked the sat nav. When they reached half a mile offshore, he wound the engines down to an idle. Pulling a powerful pair of binoculars out of the storage box in the RIB's steering console, he scanned the horizon. Satisfied they were far enough from prying eyes he turned to the crew at the back of the boat.

'Get him in, Al,' he shouted.

Allen Crow and Bill Knoff peeled the tarpaulin off to reveal Robert Farley's pale corpse laying on top of half a dozen large canvas holdalls. Slade had drowned him in the sea last night but couldn't leave him on the beach with all the tyre tracks and DNA from him and his team scattered all over the place. They dragged him to the side of the boat and slid him gently into the sea. Slade watched him float away, then waited for Allen to secure the tarpaulin over the holdalls before checking his diver's watch and pushing the throttles forward again. The crew held on tight as the boat headed further out to sea, bouncing over the gentle swell.

'Gotta get a move on, Des, we're behind,' he said, checking the satellite position.

'Don't worry, guv, we'll be there on slack tide and be away before it's running fast,' said Des smiling back.

Slade was in no smiling mood. The strangers in the car park had rattled him and he wasn't happy about the heat the couple on the beach were drawing by their disappearance .

CHAPTER 9

Barney Stock was back in the observation room leering at Susan Wimple. He'd been waiting for Craig to haul his long streak of piss body up the stairs for ages. Now he was alone with her. Scared and disorientated from the drugs he'd put in her water, she'd held off from using the stainless steel toilet in the cell's corner for as long as she could. Now, with the baby pressing on her bladder, she was forced to go.

'That's right, darlin', show us what you've got,' Barney said in a breathless whisper, his hand down, rubbing his crotch.

Each observation room had two monitors, one showing the recorder image of the cell in front, the other displaying a grid of images: one for each cell, the room between them and the hay barn above. Barney glanced across when movement in one of the other cells caught his eye.

'What the fuck?' he said, tapping the keyboard to bring up cell two. His eyes went wide at the sight of Smudge convulsing on the floor.

Shit.

Moving his stocky frame as fast as he could, he left the observation room and ran for the cell door, fumbling and rattling a big bunch of keys as he went, desperately trying to find the right one before he got to the door.

Fuck, shit, fuck, Slade will kill me if he loses this one before the hunt.

He slid the metal flap to look in and hurriedly unlocked the door at the sight of Smudge still fitting on the floor.

'Keep breathing, mate, I'm going to put you in a recovery position, alright? Can you hear me?' he said kneeling beside Smudge.

The second he leaned over him, Smudge grabbed the collar of Barney's jacket with both hands and pulled him in while throwing his head forward with all his might. The resulting headbutt crushed Barney's nose and knocked him clean out. Blinking and seeing stars himself, Smudge got to his feet and swayed a little.

'Fucking 'ave some of that, you bastard,' he shouted at the unconscious Barney, giving him a hard kick to the bollocks just for good measure.

Moving cautiously out into the central area, Smudge took in the ten cells lining the walls.

What the fuck is this? This isn't drug smuggling; this is some sick shit.

His thoughts were broken by the sound of a woman crying for help from the cell next door, while someone hammered at a door on the other side. He thought about trying to let them all out but knew that with his background he'd have a better chance of getting out and finding help if he was alone. Moving to the concrete stairs, all he could see at the top were steel girders and heavy wooden boards. Seeing the industrial box with a green button on the wall, Smudge pressed it. There was a hum of electric motors and the hatch slid smoothly back, revealing the inside of the barn and a welcome cool breeze of fresh air.

Smudge climbed the stairs, keeping low behind the Portakabin at the top. Crossing to the barn door in double quick time, he scanned the farmyard outside. He could hear engine noise somewhere close by but couldn't see it. It was something small: a motorbike or a quad bike. Seeing the farm track leading off into the woods, Smudge decided to make a break for it and follow the track to the main road. With the adrenaline pumping through his veins, he ran full pelt, heading for the track, only stopping once he got past the tree line. Flattening himself behind a large pine tree, Smudge sucked in great gulps of air to slow his pounding heart.

I should've hit the gym like Danny, he'd be in fucking London by now.

When his breathing was under control, Smudge set off up the track. He ran steadily, scanning the way ahead, ready to head into the trees at the first sign of trouble. He got about a mile down the track when he heard the engine sound again.

Wait, now there are two of them.

Smudge headed into the trees about thirty metres, then turned to run parallel to the track. Somewhere further back he could hear the vehicles heading up the track. Picking up the pace, Smudge flew through the trees, ignoring the small branches that whipped across his face as he went. The sound of the engines changed direction, then split. One was somewhere over to the left, on the track; the other one was somewhere behind him, revving as it manoeuvred around the trees. Quad bikes, he was sure of it. Changing tactic, Smudge ran deeper into the woods, then turned to head in the direction he hoped would be the main road.

The engine noise seemed quieter, giving him hope of a greater distance between them and him. With lungs bursting and his heart fit to burst too, he slid on his arse and threw himself back against a tree to recover. Forcing himself to calm down, Smudge leaned his head back against the tree with his eyes closed and listened to the sound of the quads. He realised he could only hear one now somewhere over to his right. Opening his eyes ready for the next sprint, something high in the tree in front of him caught his eye. To his surprise, a small section of twigs and leaves spun round to expose a camera lens. It tilted down, looking straight at him.

Fuck, they've been tracking me all the time.

Exploding into action, Smudge went all out towards what he hoped was the edge of the estate and a main road to freedom. The sound of the quad grew louder to his left, but he ignored it. Powering through the pain in his body, Smudge broke the tree line into a meadow. A hundred metres ahead of him lay the boundary wall with the main road beyond. He got within thirty feet of the wall when a sharp pain like a hundred wasp stings bit him in the back of the leg. Sliding to the floor on his front, he twisted to see a dart sticking out. He tried to get to his feet, but his legs were already turning to jelly. Within seconds his head spun and darkness consumed him. Two quad bikes appeared out of the tree line, bouncing across the meadow to stop by Smudge's side.

Dressed in a full one-piece camouflaged hunting suit, Craig took the tranquilliser gun off his shoulder and kept it pointed at Smudge. On the other side of him, Barney climbed painfully off his quad. His balls hurt like hell and he had tissue stuffed up his broken nose to stop the bleeding.

'Check he's out for the count,' Craig said nodding to Barney.

Moving in, Barney kicked Smudge hard in the side. When he didn't move, Craig propped the gun up against his quad and pulled a roll of gaffer tape out from the storage pocket under the seat. He hog-tied Smudge up with the tape, then glared at Barney.

'Help me get him on the rack. When we get him back, you make yourself scarce. I suggest we don't tell Slade. He'll lose his shit if he find out about this.'

'It wasn't my fault,' Barney complained as he picked up Smudge's legs.

They lay Smudge over the large rack fixed to the back of Craig's quad, then both mounted their bikes.

'Well, it sure as hell isn't mine, is it? Fuck it, let's just get him back, ok?'

Barney decided not to push the point and just nodded before they both bounced slowly across the meadow before

joining the farm track and disappearing through the woods.

CHAPTER 10

The RIB chugged along at a couple of knots just over ten miles off the coast. It was a good day: they'd hit slack tide and the sea was calm. Slade leaned over the side turning a radio tag finder on its pole while looking at the direction screen mounted on top. Des watched from the wheel, steering to Slade's directions.

'Switch her off, Des,' said Slade, nodding to Allen who threw the shot line in to mark the dive sight.

Bill and Allen quickly kitted up, double checking each other's kit before rolling backwards off the RIB into the sea. They swam to the buoy floating at the top of the shot line. After a thumbs up, they let the air out of their BCD and disappeared below the surface.

'How much this time?' said Des casually.

'Same as last, 50 kilos,' said Slade, as if they were talking about a grocery delivery.

'Except last time we only had 49 when we unloaded it.'

'And we'll get the missing one back. I'm not letting Sir John-fucking-Riddlesworth take twenty large out of our end,' Slade said, a flash of anger crossing his face.

'Smith must have hidden it in that shitty little chalet somewhere,' Des said, thinking out loud.

'We'll look for it tonight, just me and you, ok?'

'Ok guv.'

The conversation stopped as two Aqualung lifting bags broke the surface twenty feet away from the RIB. Des manoeuvred the boat in close, then helped Slade drag the lifting bags and heavy identical canvas holdalls to the ones under the tarpaulin into the boat.

As the sea water drained out of the canvas, Slade unzipped the holdalls one by one, checking the plastic-wrapped packages of cocaine as he hunted for the marine radio transmitter. He found it in the third bag and fished it out, checking the yellow plastic device's battery level and blinking green transmission light. Satisfied the level was good, he placed it to one side and zipped the bags back up. Leaving them where they were, he and Des moved over to the back of the RIB and pulled the tarpaulin to one side. They dragged the dry canvas bags forward out of the way and fetched the wet bags full of drugs, piling them in the dry bags' places before covering them with the tarpaulin.

Slade unzipped one of the dry canvas holdalls and checked the vacuum-sealed plastic bags containing fat bundles of used twenty-pound notes. He slid the yellow plastic transmitter in and zipped it back up again. Meanwhile, Des was huffing and puffing as he shuffled a heavy steel anchor down from the front of the boat. They threaded a rope through the handles on the holdalls and the eye of the anchor, tying the ends securely together. A few metres away, Bill and Allen broke the surface near the buoy and swam over. Slade and Des helped them on board, leaving them to stow their diving kit while they hefted the money bags and anchor over the side. They sank fast, fading into the inky black sea until all they could see was a stream of rising bubbles as the air worked its way out of the holdalls.

'That'll keep Lars happy for another week,' said Slade, moving back up to the centre console.

'I wouldn't want to be around if the Dutchman wasn't happy,' said Des giving Slade a knowing look.

'That makes two of us,' replied Slade winding up the throttle and powering the RIB towards the shore.

CHAPTER 11

When they left the snack bar for the second time that morning, Danny and Fergus hovered around the amusement arcade and shops until the tractor returned from towing a jet skier to the water's edge.

'I fancy his job, getting paid to tow all the boats across the sand all day, topping up your tan and eyeing up all the talent,' said Fergus jovially.

'One, you'd get bored, Ferg. Two, your missus would cut your knackers off if she caught you eyeing up the talent,' said Danny with a big grin.

'Fair point. Let's see what the local yokel's got to say for himself,' Fergus replied, heading for the car park.

The driver parked his tractor in his own bay at the far side of the car park. He was what they called a good old boy in Norfolk speak. Somewhere around fifty, Norfolk born and bred, and probably came out of the womb on a John Deere tractor.

'Alright, mate?' said Danny with a welcoming smile.

'Arr,' said the driver looking at him sideways with obvious dislike.

'Eh, we're looking for a friend of ours, he's been diving around here, and we need to find him. His mother's sick, you see,' Fergus said with a rather unconvincing bit of bullshit.

Both Danny and the driver turned and stared at Fergus, who just shrugged after a second or two.

'Fuck it, listen, mate. This is a picture of our buddy, have you ever seen him?' Danny said showing him a photo of Smudge on his phone.

The wily old man leaned in slowly to have a look. To Danny's irritation, he stood there staring at it for what seemed like an eternity.

'Maybe I 'as, maybe I ain't.'

Resisting the urge to slap the cantankerous old git around the head, Danny slid his wallet out of his pocket and pulled out a twenty. The old man's eyes followed the note greedily.

'Let me think, I do recall someone like that. My memory's not what it used to be,' he said, looking up at the sky as he pretended to try to remember.

'Jesus. Alright, do you remember now?' Danny said, pulling another twenty out.

'Now I remember, he was with those marine biologist guys with the flash RIB and expensive gear,' he said, pinching the top of Danny's forty quid to take it.

Holding the money tight, Danny leaned in. His face hardened and his eyes bore into the man with an intense stare.

'What do you know about these guys?'

'Not a lot. I hear they're marine biologists, studying environmental changes in the seabed, global warming and pollution, and all that type of thing. They're staying at

Harrington Farm up the coast road, on the Lessingham Hall estate,' he said taking the money as Danny released it, leaving him standing there a little unnerved.

'Now that wasn't hard, was it?' Danny said moving away with Fergus.

When they were out of earshot of the driver, Danny turned to Fergus. 'His mother's sick, what the fuck was that?' he said, chuckling.

'What? I was improvising,' Fergus replied, enjoying the banter.

'Yeah, I think you need to work on that one. What say you and me go take a look at Harrington Farm while the boys are all at sea?' Danny said with a mischievous grin.

'Sounds good to me,' replied Fergus.

The two of them walked along the road, following the land side of the dunes. It left the village and went between the different holiday homes and cobbled-together chalets of various sizes and budgets. As they approached the chalet, the sound of fast-approaching cars turned their heads. The lead car was a plain silver Ford Mondeo. Its headlights flashed in time with the bright blue pulsating lights behind the grill. The car behind was a regular police car, blue lights flashing, followed by a blast of siren for good measure. Danny and Fergus turned and faced them, an unimpressed look on both their faces.

'So, what do you think this is about?' said Fergus as both cars skidded to a halt, effectively blocking them on the drive.

'Smudge said they own the police. Whatever happens, keep shtum, mate. I'll deal with this,' said Danny, fixing the first police officer with an unnerving stare that made him falter in his steps. The doors opened on the plain Mondeo and two suited men got out. They wasted no time in thrusting police ID badges in their faces.

'I'm DCI Nick Taylor and this is DC Graham Pilkington. I'd like both of you to accompany us to the police station and assist us with our enquiries,' said DCI Taylor, while the two uniformed officers moved behind them.

'Enquiries regarding what?' Danny said, his voice calm and neutral.

'With the disappearance of Robert Farley and Susan Wimple. Now we can do this calmly or I can read you your rights and arrest you,' replied DCI Taylor.

Danny could sense the two officers behind them getting ready to pounce with their cuffs out. Without a word, Danny walked towards the car with Fergus close behind him. DC Pilkington opened the back door of the Mondeo for them, slamming it shut after they got in.

As the cars drove away, Danny and Fergus relaxed back into the seat, barely taking any notice of DCI Pilkington's eyes constantly checking them out in the rear-view mirror. They drove in silence for around twenty minutes along slow, bumpy, windy country lanes, eventually entering the quiet Norfolk market town of North Walsham. A few minutes later they pulled into the police station, a modern set of buildings built behind the small, square, original police station from 1903. They pulled into the car park at the rear and followed the two detectives into the modern part of the building.

'They'll split us up, Ferg. Jerk their chain for a while, mate, while I figure out what's going on,' Danny said under his breath.

Fergus just gave a small nod as Pilkington brought them to a stop by the custody sergeant's check-in desk.

'Name,' said the officer on the desk to Danny.

'Roger Freeman,' said Danny using an old alias.

'And your address, Mr Freeman?'

'265 Walthamstow High Street.'

'Interview Room One,' the sergeant said to the police officers behind them.

'This way, sir,' one of them said, leading Danny off down the corridor. Behind him, he heard Fergus telling the custody sergeant he was Sean Connery, which made him smile.

They entered the bare interview room with its bolted down table and barred windows. Danny sat down and the officers left him, locking the door behind them. Danny slouched down and made himself comfortable. He knew how they worked.

And now they'll make me wait for a while, get me all worried and anxious.

Smiling at the thought, he crossed his arms, slid down a little further in the chair, yawned, closed his eyes and dozed off.

CHAPTER 12

Forty minutes later the sound of the interview room door being unlocked kicked Danny from dozing to wide awake in a heartbeat. He remained motionless with his eyes shut, only opening them slowly when DC Pilkington kicked his chair leg on his way past.

'Oi, wake up,' he said, taking a seat on the other side of the table and leaning in, giving Danny a look that was intended to unnerve him.

DCI Taylor walked in behind him and quietly sat down. He placed a thin, newly-created file on the desk, giving Danny a brief smile as he clicked his pen and opened it.

Ok, we've established who's good cop, bad cop. Knock yourselves out, boys.

'So you think you're some kind of comedian, do you? We know your name's not Roger Freeman, and the address you gave us is a Pizza Express outlet. Now stop pissing about and start talking,' DC Pilkington said, his voice raised.

'As far as I was aware, I'm not under arrest and I'm just

helping you with your enquiries. So why don't *you* stop pissing about and tell me what it is you want,' Danny replied calmly, adding a smile on the end to wind Pilkington up.

The vein on the side of DC Pilkington's temple pulsed and his face reddened. He was just about to come in hard when DCI Taylor came in on the conversation.

Here comes the good cop.

'Ok, let's all calm down a bit. Graham, why don't you go and get us a coffee? Would you like one, Mr …?'

'Pearson. Daniel Pearson. White, one sugar,' Danny said, giving up his real name. He was pretty sure they already knew one of them was him from his car registration.

'Pearson, great. That wasn't so hard, was it?' said DCI Taylor smiling. Pilkington got up, overdoing the scowl as he left the room.

'Now, Mr Pearson, as I said before, we are investigating the disappearance of a young couple from Sea Palling beach sometime around eleven thirty last night. We know from the camera above the chip shop that you arrived after their disappearance, at around 2:30 a.m. We also know you were asking around the village about the disappearance of Darren Smith. The reason you're here is that Mr Smith was last seen on the beach half an hour before the couple disappeared and we would very much like to talk to him ourselves. What we don't know is where Darren Smith is now, and what your relation to him would be.'

Danny took a second before answering. 'He's an old friend. We were just meeting up for a reunion. When we got here he was gone, that's all I know,' he said with a shrug.

'Old friend, old military friend?' said DCI Taylor, probing further.

'Something like that,' Danny said, reluctant to share further.

'Mr Smith is a prime suspect in this case. We would also like to talk to him about a disturbance in Reefs Bar public house where he started an unprovoked fight with some locals, putting one of them in hospital. In short, Mr Smith is bad news. My suggestion to you and your friend is to pack up, go home, and leave the detecting to us. If Mr Smith tries to contact you, call us. Ok?' Said DCI Taylor sliding a business card across the table to Danny.

As Danny picked it up, DC Pilkington entered the room, cursing when hot coffee spilled over his hand. He plonked the cardboard cups carelessly down on the table causing them to splash over the top, covering the table surface with tiny coffee puddles.

'Well?' DC Pilkington said, still overdoing the tough guy routine.

'Mr Pearson and his friend are going to return home and let the police conduct their investigation. Isn't that right, Mr Pearson?' said DCI Taylor, still keeping up the mild-mannered approach.

Danny gave a small nod and picked up his coffee cup, taking a swig without saying a word.

'Excellent. I think that concludes our business for today. I'll arrange for a uniform to drop you back at the chalet, so you can pack and be on your way,' said DCI Taylor standing and extending his hand to Danny.

Draining the lukewarm sludge that somehow passed as coffee, Danny extended his hand and shook it. They escorted him back out of the station where he found Fergus waiting for him.

'Thank you for your cooperation, gentleman. These two officers will take you back,' said DCI Taylor before disappearing back inside.

Sitting in the back of the police car, Danny and Fergus remained silent the whole journey. They waited until the police car drove away before finally speaking.

'How was it for you, Ferg?' said Danny, still following the police car with his eyes.

'That arsehole Pilkington's got a hard-on about Smudge,' Fergus replied in a matter-of-fact tone.

'Yep. Did he keep going on about us packing up and leaving them to it?' said Danny, turning towards his car.

'Only about a dozen times. Are we going home?' asked Fergus.

'Nope. The pub,' said Danny bluntly.

'Now you're talking,' Fergus replied with a big grin.

CHAPTER 13

The harsh light in the cell hurting his eyes, followed by pain in his side, followed by the urge to vomit, were the first things Smudge felt as the drug wore off. He rolled to one side on the bed and threw up violently on the floor. Breathing heavily, he lay there for a minute, the electrical pulses trying their best to fire to the parts of his brain that could make sense of it all. They hit their target with a jolt. Escape, running, woods, and the dart in the leg played out in double-quick time.

Fuck.

Struggling against the pain in his side, he sat upright. Standing on shaky legs, Smudge made his way to the stainless steel sink bolted to the wall. He splashed his face and drank the taste of bile away. Feeling much better, he turned and walked up to the one-way mirror glass. Leaning in until his face was inches away, Smudge stared defiantly as if he could see through to the other side. Inside the observation room, Barney stood inches off the glass, mirroring Smudge with a hateful stare. In an explosion of movement, Smudge slammed his palm into the glass with a deafening boom. The noise and movement made Barney jump back out of his skin. On the other side of the glass, as if he could see him, Smudge backed off grinning before turning and sitting back down on the bed.

'Fucker, I'll fucking have you for that,' Barney muttered, his pulse racing and ego dented.

Shaking it off, he left the room and went to a small kitchen fitted under the stairs. Pulling a sandwich and bottle of orange juice out of the fridge, he moved to Susan Wimple's cell. He slid the hatch open and stared at her as she shrank back on the bed, terrified at the cold hard eyes looking at her through the hatch. The locks clunked and the door swung slowly open. Susan started shaking her head and whimpering as Barney's stocky body moved into the room.

'Come on, it's alright, I ain't going to hurt you. Look, I've brought you some food and a drink,' Barney said, smiling disarmingly, but failing to hide the lecherous glint twinkling in his eyes.

'Let me go, please, I won't tell anyone. I just want to see my boyfriend, I want to see Robert,' she said, tears running down her cheeks.

Barney moved over and sat beside her, 'It's ok, I'll help you. Here, eat,' he said, smiling reassuringly.

Slowly she reached out a shaky hand and took the sandwich. Moving it to her mouth she took a small bite followed by a bigger one as hunger drove her on.

'There, that's better, isn't it?' said Barney, placing a clammy hand on her thigh.

She froze as he drew it up towards her crotch. Panicking, she shrieked and grabbed his wrist feebly, trying to push him away. Getting off on her helplessness, Barney moved his powerful arm up and grabbed her around the throat, pushing her flat on the bed. He grabbed her breast with his other hand and moved his face close to hers before taking a slow lick up her cheek.

'Barney, get off her! For fuck's sake, are you mad? Slade'll cut your balls off if he finds out,' yelled Craig from the door.

Barney reluctantly moved off her while continuing his menacing stare. He kept his hand on her throat as he moved away, only releasing his grip at the very last moment.

'I'll catch up with you later, sweetness. Oh, and don't waste your time thinking about your boyfriend. He's dead,' said Barney, just before slamming the cell door shut.

In the plush bar at the Royal Norfolk Golf Course, Lord Bartholomew Harrington-Smythe, Sir John Riddlesworth and barrister Richard Cain belly laughed over-loudly, not caring who it annoyed or disturbed. They were the rich, the elite, and could do whatever the hell they liked. Barty's phone rang just after he barked another drinks order at the long-suffering barman who did as he was told, smiling on the outside as he always did.

'Lord Harrington-Smythe,' Barty bellowed down the phone.

'Barty, it's Peter. I've got news for you,' came Peter Metcalf's apologetic voice.

'Peter, don't take all day, spit it out, man,' said Barty impatiently.

'The two men asking after Darren Smith will not be a problem, we've warned them off. They're leaving.'

'Excellent, Peter. Just close the couple's disappearance as accidental death by drowning and you'll have earned your little treat,' said Barty knowing Metcalf's perverted little mind would be doing somersaults at the thought.

'Yes, Barty, of course. Thank—'

Barty hung up on him before he had time to finish.

'The hunt is on, gentlemen. To the Sport of Kings,' he boomed, raising his glass.

'Sport of Kings,' Sir John and Richard said loudly, following Barty's lead with a raucous laugh.

'It's going to be a good month, Barty. The shipment will be on its way to the London boys and I've primed the clients to pay for the hunt,' said Sir John, his mind crunching the numbers.

'It will, old boy. You'll be able to buy another country estate at this rate. I hear Suffolk's very nice,' said Barty, setting them all off with overly loud laughter once again.

CHAPTER 14

Danny and Fergus drove the short distance to the village, passing the main car park and the tractor still ferrying boats across the soft sand to the sea and back. They turned into the village and paid a few quid to a guy using his small field as a private car park. Leaving the car they walked down towards the access ramp to the beach. Danny spotted the tractor driver bringing the diving club's RIB back in from their morning dive. He tapped Fergus on the arm and headed over towards him.

'Oi, Worzel, have the marine bio guys returned yet?' said Danny, not in the mood for a repeat game of trying to get an answer out of the cagey local.

'Mmm, let me think, 'ave I seen em?' he replied, still looking shiftily out of the corner of his eye.

'Listen, pal, I've had a pretty shitty day so far and you really don't want to know what's going to happen if you don't give me a straight answer,' said Danny, his face hard as granite and his eyes dark and menacing as they bore into him.

'Alright, no need to get your knickers in a twist. They

should be back soon,' he said turning and climbing back into the tractor's cab, muttering something about bloody Londoners as he closed the door.

'Now I really need a pint,' said Danny, walking off towards Reefs Bar.

'You need to relax, mate. It's not as if we've got a missing mate, drug dealers and bent police to deal with, is it?' said Fergus, breaking out into a cheesy grin.

'Thanks, Ferg, I feel so much better now,' Danny said, returning his friend's good humour.

They walked into the pub, moving through the holiday makers from one of the caravan parks nearby and day-trippers visiting the beach. Danny waited patiently at the bar, letting a lady go ahead of him so she got the young woman serving and he caught the older man who had the look of the landlord about him.

'Two pints of Stella please,' Danny said, waiting until the man returned before asking him some questions. 'Excuse me, buddy, we're trying to find an old mate of ours, Darren Smith, goes by the name Smudge, we've been told he drinks in here?'

'Smudge, yeah, he comes in here a few times a week. He's usually with Vincent Slade and the marine biology lot staying up at Harrington Farm. They'll probably be in tonight, they usually do after a dive,' said the landlord with a smile.

'Thanks, he gets a bit lively after a few drinks. I hope he hasn't caused you any grief,' said Danny, handing over a tenner.

'No, he's been good as gold, although I saw him arguing with Vincent out the front the other night. Don't know what about.'

'Thanks, pal,' Danny said, taking the change off him.

Shuffling through the busy pub, they found a table

looking out at the road and day-trippers going up and down the access ramp to the beach.

'So much for Smudge smashing up the place and putting someone in hospital, like Pilkington and Taylor said,' said Fergus, gulping down a big mouthful of drink.

'Proves they are on the payroll. Time's short, Ferg. If we're going to get Smudge back we need something to bargain with,' Danny said gazing out the window, deep in thought.

'Do you think he's still alive?'

'Have to, Ferg. Until we know otherwise, we have to,' said Danny, craning his neck to see a police 4x4 and a black coroner's van coming over the ramp from the beach. They disappeared out of sight up Beach Road. Danny and Fergus swung their heads back at the sound of a chugging diesel engine. An orange vehicle, like a digger without the bucket on the front, came into view towing an orange solid-hulled boat with *Sea Palling Independent Lifeboat* written on it.

'Hold tight, Ferg, I'm just going to find out what's going on,' said Danny, already up out of his seat.

Weaving his way out of the pub, Danny walked casually up to one of the lifeboat crew following behind the lifeboat up the ramp.

'I see the coroner's van. There been a bad one?'

'Yeah, a couple went missing last night, and the boyfriend washed up on the beach earlier. We've searched the area but couldn't find his girlfriend. She's pregnant as well. Terrible business,' the crewman said, shaking his head.

Danny returned to the pub and sat back down.

'It—it's not Smudge, is it?' said Fergus, hardly daring to ask.

'No, it's one of the couple that disappeared last night, the boyfriend.'

'Shit, I don't know whether to feel happy or sad about that, mate.'

They sat chatting for about an hour and had just finished their second pint when the tractor chugged past towing an empty trailer towards the beach. They sat and waited for what seemed like ages until the sound of the chugging diesel engine grew louder and the tractor passed the pub window with the large 30-foot RIB in tow. Slade and the crew trudged past behind it with their wetsuits peeled down to their waists.

'Once they get round the corner, we'll go get the car. I want to follow these fuckers and see where they go,' said Danny, draining his pint.

'Lead the way, my man,' said Fergus, banging the empty glass on the table.

CHAPTER 15

Being late afternoon, most of the day-trippers had left and the private car park was less than half-full. Danny moved his car over to a space near the road, giving them an unobstructed view of Slade and his men as they hitched the RIB trailer onto the Mercedes. They watched as two of the crew stood in the boat, passing diving kit down to the others who loaded it into the back of the Nissan pickup trucks. While the crew moved equipment about, a gust of wind blew up the corner of the tarpaulin, giving Danny and Fergus a fleeting glimpse of the large canvas holdalls underneath.

'A fiver says that's not diving kit in those bags,' said Fergus, leaning forward in his seat to get a better view.

'I'll pass on that one, Ferg, I don't like the odds,' Danny replied, watching the men in the boat with hawk-like eyes as they quickly tied the tarpaulin down.

It only took ten minutes for the gang to load up and strip out of their wetsuits into jeans and jumpers. Climbing into the vehicles, the two pickups drove out of the car park, closely followed by the Mercedes towing the RIB.

'Here we go, Ferg,' said Danny, easing the BMW M4 out of the car park.

Due to the size of the boat, it was being towed slowly along the country road. With no fear of losing them, Danny hung way back, the powerful car barely above tick-over as it gurgled along. Five or six miles on, the convoy of vehicles swung round to follow the sea on one side and a long estate wall on the other. Far ahead of them the trailer's brake lights flashed, and the lead pickup peeled off left through the estate wall, heading off down a farm track before disappearing into woods. The other two vehicles continued on straight. As Danny and Fergus got level with the turning, they looked down the farm track to see the Nissan's lights turning on through the trailing dust cloud as it drove on from the dwindling daylight into the darkness of the shadowy woods.

'I wonder what's down there,' Danny said more to himself than to Fergus.

They continued on for about a mile with the RIB just visible in the distance, before passing a beaten-up dented Ford Mondeo wedged firmly in the ditch on the side of the road.

'Isn't that Smudge's car?' said Fergus, craning his neck to get a good look at it as they passed.

'Yeah, it looks like it. We must be getting close to Harrington Farm.'

Barely a mile further on, they could see a large, red-bricked farmhouse behind rows of trees. The trailer's indicators blinked and both the Nissan and the Mercedes towing the RIB turned down a long gravel drive that curled round through the trees, disappearing out of sight behind the farmhouse. Moments later Danny cruised straight past. He kept going until he found a layby about half a mile down the road and pulled in.

'Up for a bit of reconnaissance?' Danny said with a grin.

'You try stopping me,' said Fergus, getting out of the car in a flash.

'Hang on a sec,' said Danny, popping the boot up.

With the daylight almost gone, Danny opened up a large red toolbox and rummaged around under the dim boot light.

'Here, hold this,' he said, handing Fergus a large Maglite torch while he delved back into the toolbox.

He found the little leather pouch he was looking for and shut the toolbox and boot down.

'What you got in there?' asked Fergus.

'Lock picks. I was going for the subtle approach rather than kick any door down and wake the neighbours.'

'Fuck me, that's a first,' said Fergus, following Danny over the wall.

The two of them crossed the small strip of grass by the layby, vanishing into the woods that surrounded the farmhouse. Even though it had been a few years since they were in the SAS, the two of them fell into a natural awareness of each other and their surroundings. They moved low at a steady pace around five metres apart. As they got closer to the farmhouse, they could see a barn beyond a heavily floodlit courtyard. This made their approach easier as the powerful halogen lamp blinded anyone trying to see into the darkness of the woods beyond. Moving down the side of the barn, they got lower and slower as they approached the front. They could hear multiple voices ahead of them and moved behind a stack of fifty or so pallets stacked beside the barn to get a view of the courtyard.

They could see a large, white, refrigerated van ahead of them. Its rear doors were open showing them the floor-to-ceiling racks full of white plastic trays. On the concrete floor behind the van, Allen and Bill were busy unzipping the large canvas bags and lining rows of empty plastic trays with sealed blocks of cocaine. In the back of the van, a tall, thickset guy in a bomber jacket and gloves was dragging a big dustbin toward the back. He hopped down, grabbed the dustbin with both hands and heaved it down onto the concrete with a thud.

'Right, that's the lot, Bill, cover 'em up,' said Allen, collecting the empty canvas bags up before disappearing into the barn with them.

While the guy hopped back into the van, Bill tipped the dustbin over and shook a steady stream of ice into the plastic trays covering the cocaine bricks.

'Oi, numbnuts, don't fill them up too much, I've gotta get the fish in yet.'

'Alright, Ken, keep your fucking hair on,' grumbled Bill as Ken brought trays of fresh cod and plaice down and shared them out into the trays on the floor.

'Cover them up, Bill,' Ken said, returning to the back of the van.

Allen returned from the barn as Bill emptied the last of the ice from the dustbin. He passed the empty bin up to Ken in the van, then he and Allen started sliding the trays into the back of the van where Ken put them in the racks. When they'd finished, Ken hopped down and swung the doors shut, exposing *Riddlesworth Fish Merchants, Chelsea* sign-written across them.

'That's me done, I'll see you next week,' Ken said, climbing into the cab and starting it up.

As he turned round in the courtyard and left, Slade and Des came out of the farmhouse and headed over to the Mercedes.

'We're going out, Bill. Lock the barn up then message the Dutchman. Tell him the money's at the drop. He can get it tomorrow at low tide,' said Slade climbing into the Mercedes with Des and driving off without waiting for Bill to answer.

'Yes sir, I'll stick a broom up my arse and sweep the floor while I'm at it,' Bill grumbled under his breath.

'Watch it, Bill, you push Slade too hard and you'll find yourself in the hunt with them other poor bastards,' said Allen.

'Bollocks, he wouldn't dare,' scoffed Bill, suddenly braver now Slade had disappeared down the road.

'Well, don't say I didn't warn you. I'm going to check on Barney and our guests. The Lord of the Manor will have his guests arriving soon,' said Allen jumping on a quad bike parked near the farmhouse. He started it up and headed off down a farm track opposite the barn.

'Yeah, ok,' shouted Bill, snapping a padlock on the barn before heading into the farmhouse.

'Busy little bastards aren't they?' whispered Fergus to Danny.

'Certainly are. Let's take a look in that barn.'

CHAPTER 16

Moving to the front of the barn, Danny slipped the little pouch of lock picks out of his pocket and went down on one knee. Fergus stood with his back to him. His eyes firmly fixed on the farmhouse as Danny manoeuvred the picks around in the heavy padlock, feeling and manipulating one pin after another.

'Come on, what's taking so long? My granny could pick that quicker than you,' whispered Fergus, expecting people to come running out of the farmhouse at any second.

'Hang on, I'm a bit rusty, mate. Wait, got it,' Danny said, clicking the lock open.

He slid the door open just enough for them to slip inside, easing it shut behind them.

'Give us some light, Ferg.'

'Er, oh, right,' replied Fergus, pulling the Maglite out of his pocket and turning it on. The powerful beam lit up the front of the RIB looming over them on its trailer.

'Give it here, I'm going up,' said Danny, taking the torch.

He moved down the side of the boat and agilely leaped up into it at the rear where it was lower to the ground.

'So, what are we looking for?' said Fergus, watching Danny move to the steering console.

'You heard them, Ferg, they pick up the drugs from a dive site and drop the money for some Dutch bloke. Do me a favour and google what time high tide is tonight,' said Danny, his face illuminating as he turned on the boat's sat nav.

'I still don't get it,' said Fergus, tapping away on his phone.

'Bingo, we're going night fishing, Ferg,' replied Danny, taking a picture on his phone of the last used longitude and latitude in the sat nav's log.

Flashing the torch to one side, Danny spotted the marine radio tag finder lying in the bottom of the boat. He picked it up and studied it while holding the Maglite in his mouth.

'Oi! You in the boat, climb down slowly,' shouted Bill from just inside the sliding door, a Glock 17 pointed squarely at Danny's head.

At the back of the boat Fergus stepped back silently into the darkness. Danny flicked his head up, the torch in his mouth shining its powerful beam into Bill's eyes.

'Put the fucking torch down and get out of the b—'

Before Bill could get his words out, Fergus exploded out of the shadows swinging a belt full of heavy diving weights. The blow came down on the side of Bill's head, sending him to the floor. Fergus was standing over him by the time he hit the deck, ready to clock him again if he tried to get up, but he was out cold.

'Is he dead?' said Danny hopping down from the boat with the radio tag finder.

'Nah, he's still breathing,' said Fergus, picking up Bill's

dropped Glock handgun and tucking it in his jeans.

'You're losing your touch, mate. Let's tie him up and gag him. We can tuck him under the tarpaulin in the boat, might buy us and hour or two until they find him.'

Hunting around on the workbenches along the wall, they found a roll of gaffer tape and hogged-tied Bill up so tight he wouldn't be able to move a muscle when he came round. Spinning the last of the roll around his head and mouth, Danny and Fergus picked him up at each end and with a one-two-three swung him into the boat. Climbing up, they dragged Bill to the tarpaulin at the back and lifted it to roll him under. Bill's eyes opened as they pushed going wide in panic as he came round. Danny gave him a grin and a wink before pulling the tarpaulin down leaving him wriggling against the mountain of strong tape.

'Let's get out of here, we've got to get Smudge's diving kit and find a boat,' said Danny, making for the door.

'What's this then, a double-decker bus?' said Fergus, pointing at the RIB behind them.

'Well done, brains, and how are you going to get it to the sea, pull it? We don't have anything to tow it with.'

'Fair point,' Fergus said, a big grin on his face.

'I don't know how, but we'll have to get a boat from somewhere. What time is tonight's high tide?'

'Ten past one, and about that boat...'

'What about the boat?' Danny said, turning the Maglite off as they reached the door.

'I think I know where we can get one,' said Fergus, sliding the door open just enough to check the coast was clear.

They stepped out, shutting the door and snapping the padlock shut behind them. Moving back round the side of the barn, they vanished into the darkness, heading back through the woods towards the car.

CHAPTER 17

Taking the return drive at a much faster pace, Danny and Fergus pulled up outside the chalet. They got out of the car and approached the door. For the second time in 24 hours, they found it ajar. Without saying a word, they automatically peeled off to each side of the door. Fergus had Bill's Glock up and ready, safety off and finger on the trigger. Danny reached across and gently pushed the door open with the back of his hand. He took a quick look into the small, shadowy kitchen, his brain still processing the image as he pulled back out beside the door. As before, the place was dark and quiet; he still didn't get the sense anyone was inside. Signalling to Fergus to peel left into the lounge when they entered, Danny rushed in to the right to check the kitchen. Sweeping around with the gun up in front of him, Fergus passed him into the lounge. The two stood motionless in the dark, listening.

'Anything?' Danny said in a hushed voice.

'Nope, it's clear in here,' Fergus replied normally, giving up on anyone being there and flicking the light on.

Danny did the same and turned the light on in the kitchen.

'Jesus,' he said at the mess. The kitchen was turned upside down, drawers out, plates and crockery smashed all over the floor.

'Fuck me, and I thought it was a shithole before,' came Fergus's voice from the lounge.

Danny went through to join him. They'd trashed the small room, sofa cushions all slashed, the TV smashed on the floor and its cabinet upside down.

'What were they looking for?' said Fergus, tucking the gun in the back of his jeans.

Danny shook his head before the answer dawned on him. 'Shit, the brick, the fucking drugs package,' he said, rushing up the narrow stairs. He pushed the turfed-up bed out of the way and opened the airing cupboard. Sticking his hand behind the hot water tank, Danny already knew the brick would be gone. Confirming his suspicions, he turned and shook his head to Fergus as he entered the room.

'At least we know who it was, unless you know another gang of drug smugglers in this quiet seaside village,' said Fergus, standing a set of drawers upright.

'Yeah, and that's another reason why we don't want to stick around here for too long. Help me find all Smudge's diving gear under all this mess.'

They found Smudge's canvas dive bag and started filling it as they uncovered each piece of diving kit.

'So what's this plan of yours to get a boat?' Danny said, placing Smudge's breathing regulator and dive cylinder on the bed.

'I'm not sure you're going to like it, but I thought we could—'

The pair of them instantly fell quiet at the sound of movement downstairs. They flattened themselves either side of the bedroom door, Danny grabbing an overturned chair, holding it up to one side, ready to smash it down if need be. Fergus was on the other side of the door with the gun out ready. The sound of movement got louder as footsteps climbed the wooden stairs. Fergus signalled one finger for one person, then signalled to himself to take the lead when the unknown assailant entered the room. Danny nodded and remained tense with the chair in case he needed to strike. The adrenaline built with the tension as the footsteps stopped just short of the top of the stairs.

'Your missus still buying you that bloody awful aftershave then, Ferg?' came a very familiar voice.

'Yeah, and you still sound like a bull in a china shop. We heard you coming a mile off,' said Fergus, stepping forward as Charles Leman walked in through the door.

'Good to see you, brother,' said Fergus, embracing Chaz and slapping him on the back.

'And you, mate,' said Chaz, turning to Danny with a big grin on his face.

'It's been a while. How did you know we were here?' said Danny, giving him a quick hug and slap on the back.

'Oh, I returned Ferg's call and Carol told me you were up here. Man, she's pissed at you, Ferg.'

'No change there then,' laughed Fergus.

'So where's that dozy prat Smudge?'

'I'll fill you in on everything, mate, but first we need to get out of here and steal a boat,' said Danny, returning to Smudge's dive bag to shove the last of his diving kit in.

'Hang on, what? Steal a boat?' said Chaz, looking puzzled.

'It's good to see you, Chaz,' chuckled Danny passing

him Smudge's dive cylinder. 'Now, you were about to tell me about the boat, Ferg.'

'Right, well this is the plan,' said Fergus, leading them down the stairs.

CHAPTER 18

Tearing up the shingle drive, Slade bounced up onto the concrete courtyard, screeching to a stop outside Harrington Farm. As they headed for the door, Allen appeared from the farm track leading to the hay barn and cells. He parked the quad bike up near the barn and followed Slade and Des into the farmhouse.

'How's our guests, Al?' said Des, peeling a beer off a six-pack in the fridge and throwing it to him.

'Cheers. They're quiet, Barney is keeping an eye on them.'

'Where have you two been?'

'Retrieving some lost property,' said Slade, pulling the cocaine block out of his jacket and placing it in the middle of the kitchen table.

'Shit, nice one. That'll shut the fucking toffs up,' said Allen, raising his can in salute.

'Yeah, I'm going to call him now. Where's Bill?' said Slade, pulling his mobile out.

'I don't know, I left him here when I went over to the

hay barn. I'll go and see if he's upstairs,' Allen said, walking away.

Slade took a swig of beer as he watched him leave, then hit the call button and waited while it rang and rang. Lord Bartholomew always made a point of making his minions wait.

'Calling me at this time of night, this better be good,' came Barty's condescending voice.

'It is. I wanted to let you know we have recovered the missing item,' said Slade, always careful not to say anything incriminating over the phone.

'Mmm, delightful news, and what of our visitors?' said Barty, speaking deliberately slowly for effect.

'No sign of them, sir, it looks like they've already gone,' replied Slade, itching to get off the phone with Barty.

Pompous prick.

'Excellent, we can concentrate on preparations for the hunt. The clients will be arriving Monday and I want everything to be perfect for them. Goodnight, Vincent,' said Barty, hanging up without waiting for a reply, his words more of a statement rather than a request.

'Did His Right Honourableness hang up on you again?' said Des with a grin.

'Yep, one of these days I'm going to shove his title where the sun don't shine,' said Slade gruffly.

They drained their beers as Allen came back in scratching his head.

'He's not up there.'

'Where's that silly sod got to? Hang on, I'll call him,' said Des, fishing his phone out of his jacket pocket and hitting the call button.

All three of their heads turned slowly to face Bill's ringing mobile sitting on the windowsill.

CHAPTER 19

After driving a few miles down the coast to Happisburgh, Danny parked his BMW at the beach end of Beach Road. Chaz and Fergus drove past in Chaz's van, turning it round at the dead end. Danny got out and climbed into the cab, squeezing into the small two-man passenger seat next to Fergus.

'Fuck me, you've put weight on, Ferg?' said Danny, trying to get the seat belt in the clip.

'Sod off, I'm the same weight now as I was in the Regiment,' Fergus grumbled, offended.

'Bollocks,' said Chaz, chuckling as he headed back down Beach Road.

'I am!'

'If you say so,' said Danny, enjoying the banter he'd missed from the tight-knit group.

'I fucking am,' Fergus protested.

'Yeah, whatever,' said Chaz turning the van back towards Sea Palling.

They drove carefully, sticking to the speed limit as they

went, passing Smudge's family holiday chalet, which looked undisturbed for a change.

'Do you think this is a good idea?' said Chaz, pulling into the car park near the chippy.

'No. It's a fucking terrible idea,' said Danny, getting out.

'He's right, it really is a bad idea,' said Fergus, grinning as he followed Danny out of the van.

'Bloody idiots,' Chaz said, shaking his head as he got out and slid the side door open.

Danny grabbed Smudge's canvas dive bag and cylinder while Fergus reached in and pulled a collapsible telescopic set of ladders out, knocking a large lockbox off the van racking. It clanged to the ground, making Chaz jump back in a panic.

'Calm down, Chaz! A bit jumpy, aren't you?' said Fergus in surprise.

'So should you be, you just knocked a box of detonators off the shelf and the box it landed on has 10 pounds of plastic explosive in.'

'What the fuck are you doing with that?' said Fergus, edging away from the van.

'I'm a demolitions expert, you muppet. How do you think I'm going to get a 200-foot chimney down, tickle it?' Chaz said, kneeling in the back of the van so he could secure the box of detonators back on the shelf next to a bunch of remote triggers. Chaz grabbed a toolbox on the way out, slid the door shut and joined the other two.

It was after midnight and apart from a few stragglers from the pub, walking their unsteady way up towards the village and caravan parks, the place was deserted.

'We all set?' said Danny, his face serious and his eyes focused as he assessed the target.

'Yep, in and out,' said Fergus.

'Let's do it,' said Chaz.

The three of them moved to the corner of the closed chip shop. Danny poked his head around and checked the access ramp to the beach and the Sea Palling Independent Lifeboat station opposite.

'All clear, let's go. Keep your heads down until the camera's out,' Danny said, moving out with the other two close behind.

Fergus reached back for Chaz to grab the bottom of the telescopic ladder. As soon as he had a hand on it, Fergus moved ahead, pulling the ladder out in a volley of clicks as the steps locked in the open position. Swinging the light ladder up in front of him, Fergus thumped it down just short of the side of the lifeboat station and ran up the rungs. He was over halfway up before the top of the ladder hit the wall. A split-second later he was at the top, cranking the CCTV camera upwards to give a perfect view of the starry night sky.

'Camera's out,' he said, a little too loud.

'Ok, Chaz?' said Danny, not looking away from his kneeling position as he picked the door lock.

'Phone line's cut, just going for the alarm box,' Chaz said, passing behind Danny as he headed for Fergus who already had the ladder up under the security alarm box.

Dumping his toolbox on the floor, Chaz flipped the lid and grabbed a can of expansion foam. He scooted up the ladder and shoved its plastic tube through the slots on the side of the alarm box cover. He kept the nozzle pressed down until the setting foam oozed out of every gap. Taking the plastic tube out, Chaz squirted a generous ball of foam over the box's blue strobe light until he couldn't see it anymore. Satisfied, he took two steps down the ladder then jumped the rest of the way. After a quick look around to make sure they were undetected, he picked up his toolbox and followed Danny in through the newly opened door. Fergus flicked the latches and collapsed the ladder before heading inside, closing the door behind him.

Ignoring the beeping alarm panel, Danny went straight through to the boathouse. He threw the dive kit in the lifeboat and was already on the orange digger-like tow vehicle when Chaz came in.

'All good?' Danny said.

'Yeah, ignore that,' he said as the security panel went into alarm. 'It can't dial out with the phone line cut and nobody will hear anything from the alarm box outside.'

'Great, dump the toolbox in the boat and get the door open. Did you shut the door, Ferg?' Danny said as Fergus flew into the boathouse, chucking the ladder in the RIB.

'Yep, come on, let's go, go, go,' he said, leaping up into the boat with a grin.

They opened the large sliding door and Danny revved the chugging diesel engine, towing the boat and trailer out onto the beach ramp. The second it was clear, Chaz pulled the door shut and ran after them. He hopped on the back of the trailer and held onto the outboard motors as Danny bumped down onto the sandy beach. Turning a tight circle to face the slope, Danny crunched it into reverse and backed the trailer into the sea. As soon as it was far enough in for the lifeboat to float free, he turned off the engine, splashed through the water and climbed in.

Pressing the ignition, Danny fired up the engines, the sound feeling amplified in the night's silence. Pulling it back into deeper water, Danny turned the boat around and planted the throttles full forward. The boat took off, bouncing over the breaking waves before skimming smoothly over a calm sea swell.

Chaz and Fergus moved up beside him as he put the coordinates from Slade's RIB into the sat nav.

'That was easy,' said Fergus.

'Mmm, getting back in without getting nicked will be the tricky part. Let's hope nobody discovers the lifeboat missing before we get back,' Danny said, looking behind him at the quiet moonlit beach. 'Here, take the wheel, Ferg, I've gotta get Smudge's dive suit on.'

CHAPTER 20

'Is he there, Craig, yes or no?' Slade said impatiently down his mobile.

'No, boss. I haven't seen him all night.'

'What about Barney?'

'No, boss, he's standing right next to me, he hasn't seen him either,' said Craig, trying not to provoke Slade's anger.

'For fuck's sake, where is he?' growled Slade after he'd hung up. He turned his attention to Allen, the anger clear on his face, leaving Allen unsure of his next move.

'Have you tried the barn?' he said, his eyes cutting into Allen.

'There's no point, it's all secure, padlocked from the outside,' said Allen, shifting nervously from one foot to the other.

'I didn't fucking ask if there was any point, I asked you if you'd checked it.'

The kitchen fell into an uneasy silence. Slade didn't move, his unblinking stare never leaving Allen's face.

'S-s-sorry boss, I'll go and check it now, ok?' stuttered

Allen, moving across the far side of the kitchen so he didn't have to get any closer to Slade on his way out.

'What's-a-matter, guv? We've got the missing kilo back and those nosy bastards have fucked off. Bill's probably just gone off on one of his walks,' said Des from the back of the kitchen.

'No, Des, I don't like it. Too much of a coincidence. Smith, his friends sniffing about, Bill's disappearance. I've got a bad feeling about it.'

The second he'd finished talking, he could hear Allen yelling across the courtyard. They both burst out of the farmhouse and ran across the concrete towards the light coming from the open barn. When they entered, they couldn't see Allen down either side of the RIB.

'Allen!' Slade yelled.

'Up here, in the boat,' came Allen's urgent reply.

Rushing to the rear, they climbed in where it was lower to the ground. Allen was busy cutting a ton of gaffer tape off Bill in an attempt to free him. Finally releasing his limbs, Allen ripped the gaffer tape painfully off Bill's mouth.

'Argh, fuck, Allen,' he yelled, clutching his mouth with one hand while touching the lump on the side of his head where Fergus had cracked him one with the other.

'What happened?' Slade demanded.

'I was getting the firewood when I noticed the barn was unlocked. When I came in, I caught that bloke from the car park this morning up here on the boat with the radio finder. He couldn't have been alone, because while I had my gun on him someone jumped me from behind,' said Bill, as Allen helped him to his shaky feet.

'You said he had the radio finder in his hand?' Slade growled while moving around the boat looking for it. As he came to the steering console, he spotted the sat nav's screen still glowing with the dive site's co-ordinates.

'They know about the drop site,' he said as the penny dropped.

'Do you think they'll go to the police?' said Allen, staring at Slade's back as he stood at the steering console.

'No, Metcalf would have warned us, and they'd have been here already,' Slade said turning slowly, his face dark and dangerous as he fixed Des with a stare. 'Let's go and talk to Smith. I want to find out how much he told them and who these bastards are.'

'What about the dive site, the money?' Allen said.

'No one would be crazy enough to go out there and dive at night, and Lars's fishing crew will be there in the morning. We'll change the location for the next drop off,' Slade said jumping down from the boat and leaving the barn as the others followed his lead.

'Should we tell Lord Bartholomew?' said Allen, catching up with Slade.

With a lightning move, Slade spun round and grabbed Allen by the throat, slamming him back into the side of the barn.

'Ask me another stupid question, I fucking dare you,' Slade said, his face inches away from Allen's wide-eyed, scared, shaking head.

'Sorry, boss,' Allen croaked through his constricted throat.

'We don't tell the lord or Sir John shit, ok? They'll freak out and cancel the hunt, and we've all got too much money riding on it. We say nothing and deal with it,' he said, letting go of Allen and looking intently at Des and Bill.

'Yes, boss.'

'Yeah, no problem.'

'Allen,' Slade said, turning back to him.

'Of course, no problem,' Allen replied, flinching away from Slade as he got close.

'Good, now let's go and talk to Smith.'

CHAPTER 21

The bow of the boat sank low in the water as Fergus wound back the engines to a popping tick over.

'This is it, Dan,' he said.

'Cheers, Ferg. Have a play with that radio finder, Chaz, see what it does,' Danny said, doing up his buoyancy control vest and testing the breathing regulator and gauge.

'What you got in the tank?' Fergus asked.

'It's only about half full, 120 bar. Should give 25, maybe 30 minutes.'

'That's cutting it a bit fine,' Fergus said, before getting cut short by Chaz's interruption.

'Take it starboard, Ferg, slowly,' Chaz said, turning the radio finder in the water.

'Left or right, Chaz? I ain't Captain Birdseye, you know.'

'Right, it's right, you fucking idiot.'

'Alright, keep your hair on, you sound like my wife,' shouted Fergus, moving the boat slowly starboard.

'Bit more, bit more. That's it, kill the engine, it's right under us.'

Danny dropped an anchor line in. When it hit the bottom and caught, he tied the rope off to the steel bar on the console and checked the time.

It's 1:30 a.m. We're a bit late, better get a move on before the tide starts running fast.

Danny tied one end of a rope round his weight belt and gave the other to Chaz.

'Right, I'll use the anchor line to descend and ascend, you play this rope out and I'll tie it on the bags when I find them. Two tugs and you can pull them up. Ok?' Danny said, giving Chaz a grin and a slap on the shoulder.

'Roger that,' Chaz said, winking at Danny as he turned his torch on.

Adjusting his mask, Danny placed the regulator in his mouth and rolled backwards into the water. He took a few seconds for the cold water shock to wear off, then formed a circle between his thumb and forefinger in the universal diver's *ok* symbol. Letting air out of his BCD vest, Danny descended into the darkness, going hand over hand down the anchor line. With only the line and floating particles lit by the torch in the inky blackness, the only way to tell he was descending was by the ever-increasing chill as he got deeper and deeper. Concentrating on breathing slowly and calmly to conserve his oxygen, Danny fought the natural human instinct to panic in the alien underwater world. After a few minutes that felt like hours, rocks, seaweed, and the sand of the seabed loomed into the beam of the torch. Moving away from the line, Danny realised the current was picking up faster than he'd expected. He searched around, kicking his fins hard to keep in position, the powerful beam of light from his torch cutting about three metres ahead through the murky gloom. Trying to keep his direction straight in his head, he worked in circles. Time passed and he still couldn't find the bags. The tide was definitely turning, fast. Danny held on to rocks and pulled himself along to stop himself being swept away. His only comfort was the rope he had tied around his weight belt. Shining the torch on his air gauge, he was shocked to find he only had 70 bar of air left. Working against the strong current was burning through his oxygen fast.

Shit, another five minutes and I'll have to give up. I need ten minutes for the decompression stop on the way up.

Dragging himself forward with his head just above the seabed, a crab the size of a dinner plate reared its angry claws up inches from his mask, making him jump and lose grip. With the tide running ever faster, Danny travelled twenty metres in seconds, sweeping him over the mound of weighted-down money bags. Glimpsing them in his torch-light, Danny shot out his hand and caught a handle, gripping it tight before the tide swept him another twenty metres into the inky blackness.

With his air down to 40 bar, Danny worked quickly. Tying the rope from his waist through the handles of the canvas bags, he cut the anchor free that was weighing them down and gave two big tugs on the rope. A few seconds later Fergus and Chaz started pulling the load up. As Danny ascended, the bags moved closer to the boat, bringing the anchor line into view. Danny reached across and grabbed it. Letting go of the bags, he watched them float past and disappear above him. Shining the torch onto his G-Shock watch, Danny started timing his ten-minute decompression stop that would stop him getting the bends. Gripping on tight against the current, his eyes moved between his watch and air gauge. Normally he would never go below the 50 bar set aside for an emergency backup. He was down to 15 bar and still had five minutes to decompress. Relaxing all but his grip, Danny breathed as calmly as he could, while watching the seconds tick by excruciatingly slowly.

Time's up.

As he pulled himself up the anchor line, Danny could feel the air supply dwindling, forcing him to hold his breath for the last few metres until he broke the surface. Chaz and Fergus grabbed him under each armpit and hauled him into the boat.

'You took your time, I thought you'd swum back to shore,' said Fergus with a big grin on his face.

'That was a bit too close for comfort. Next time I come up with a stupid idea like that, just give me a slap, ok?' Danny said, getting his breath back.

'I'll remember that,' Fergus said, pulling in the anchor line.

'Get us back to shore, Chaz,' Danny said, unclipping the diving cylinder and vest.

'Aye, aye, captain,' Chaz shouted, punching the throttle and heading for shore.

CHAPTER 22

The harsh strip lights blinking on stirred Smudge out of his sleep. Multiple hands grabbed him, kick-starting him into wide awake. Bill, Des and Allen pulled him upright in front of Slade who powered his fist into Smudge's stomach. The blow wasn't so much painful as shocking to the body, knocking every ounce of air out of him as it disrupted his diaphragm, making it hard to breathe.

'Put him in the chair,' ordered Slade.

Des and Allen put one of Smudge's arms over each of their shoulders and took him out of the cell coughing and wheezing with his feet dragging behind him. They took him across the centre space towards a room on the opposite side to his cell. Smudge could hear a woman crying for help from the cell next to his, her voice desperate and pleading. Bill opened the door ahead of them and turned on the light. Much to Smudge's horror there was a dentist-like chair with shackles at the hands, feet, neck and waist. It was lit by a powerful light from an operating theatre. Regaining a little composure, Smudge's eyes went wide at the sight of the trolleys with surgical drills, saws, knives and instruments he couldn't even guess the use for. Blind panic and adrenaline kicked in. Smudge darted his head to one side and clamped his teeth down on Allen's ear, biting hard through the cartilage until it separated free from Allen's screaming head. As he let go, Smudge turned to Des, spitting blood and the piece of ear into Des's eyes. Letting go of Smudge in surprise, Des went to wipe his eyes but got the full force of Smudge's headbutt before he got his hands up. With his survival instincts kicking in before Des hit the floor, Smudge was on top of Bill as he fumbled to get his gun out. He kicked him in the balls, then floored him with a left hook to the temple as he bent forward in agony.

With fury and confidence rising, Smudge went for Bill's dropped gun in a race against Slade, who was moving in fast. He got a grip on the gun and was raising it to take aim when Slade did a blisteringly quick spinning kick, knocking the gun clean out of his hand. Smudge went into defensive mode, putting his arms up and taking a wide stance like a boxer. Slade exploded on him with a mixture of martial arts and boxing. Punches, knees and kicks assaulted Smudge's body and head, easily finding their way through his blocks and avoiding his jabs. As he backed away, Des cracked him on the back of the head with the side of his gun. Smudge lost balance for a second, long enough for everyone to pile on top of him, knocking him to the floor where they kicked and punched him repeatedly.

'Fuck off, fuck you, bastards,' Smudge grunted as he tried to absorb the blows.

Within minutes it was futile. Pummelled and beaten, Smudge was moving towards unconsciousness.

'Stop. Enough. Get him in the chair,' barked Slade.

Still furious, Allen continued to kick Smudge, his hand against the side of his head with blood leaking through his fingers. Slade pushed him away, throwing him a warning look. Not brave enough to challenge him, Allen backed off to find something to stop his ear bleeding. With the fight knocked out of him, Des and Bill dumped Smudge in the chair and strapped him down.

'You're really starting piss me off, Smith. Now, I'm going to ask you some questions. How you answer will decide whether or not I let Allen cut your bollocks off.'

At that point Allen came into view with a lump of wadding on his ear held in place by a fresh bandage around his head. He looked down at the equipment trolleys and picked up an electric bone saw, pulling the trigger to make it buzz menacingly.

'What did you tell your two buddies about our operation?' Slade said, leaning close to Smudge's face.

'Fuck off, your breath smells like shit,' Smudge grunted.

In a flash, Slade pulled his hunting knife out of its sheath and thumped it down into Smudge's thigh. He screamed out as the tip chipped into the bone, sending electric shocks of pain shooting through his body.

'Let's try that again, what did you tell your friends?' Slade repeated, slowly twisting the knife in Smudge's leg as he spoke.

'Argh, go fuck yourself,' Smudge grunted and gasped.

Slade's face contorted in anger. He pulled the knife out and went for Smudge's throat. Des caught his wrist and held it firm, just as the blade creased Smudge's skin.

'Boss, Sir John wants him fit for the hunt,' said Des, hoping Slade wouldn't turn on him in his rage.

Breathing heavily through his nose, it took a few seconds before the pressure against Des's grip relented and Slade pulled the blade away, leaving a trickle of blood winding its way down Smudge's neck from a nick in the skin.

'Bandage the leg and lock him back up,' said Slade, sliding the knife away before turning and walking out.

Allen leaned in close, sticking his thumb in the wound in Smudge's leg, causing him to grit his teeth and strain against the leather restraining straps.

'Think yourself lucky, boy. You'll get a sporting chance and a clean bullet to the head. The Chief is a sick bastard, he's going to cut that poor pregnant cow to pieces. She'll be begging for him to kill her by the time he's finished.'

Allen backed away, leaving Smudge staring at him with an intense hatred. Grabbing Smudge's hair, Des pulled his head to one side and jabbed a syringe into his neck. Before he could jerk away and pull against the restraints, Smudge's head started spinning. He felt like he was getting dragged backwards into a black tunnel. The room shrank to a dot in the distance and he fell unconscious.

CHAPTER 23

'Are we close?' Danny shouted to Chaz over the roar of the outboard engines.

'About a mile from Happisburgh Lighthouse,' Chaz shouted looking over his shoulder at Danny, who was shoving the last of Smudge's diving kit into the canvas bag. His eyes wandered off the back of the boat, settling on a light in the sky, far off in the distance. He stared at it for a few seconds before the penny dropped.

'Danny, we've got company,' he shouted back, pointing to the helicopter's searchlight in the distance.

'Shit, can we get any more speed out of this thing?' said Danny, moving up to the steering console.

'A little, if we redline the engines.'

'Do it,' Danny said, looking back as Chaz pushed the throttle fully open, causing the engines to scream even louder. They'd headed back from the dive site on a different course, taking them a few miles away from Sea Palling and a mile or so away from Happisburgh and Danny's parked up BMW.

'Come on, come on,' Danny said, watching the helicopter zig-zagging over the sea, its powerful searchlight sweeping its way across the water, working closer towards them.

The three of them held on tight as the lifeboat buffeted across the waves as they powered along, parallel to the beach.

'There, over there, the path up to Beach Road,' shouted Fergus.

Chaz and Danny turned, spotting the houses and streetlights near Danny's car before turning back to the helicopter's closing search pattern.

'It's going to be close,' said Chaz.

'Don't slow down, hit the beach full speed,' Danny said as they passed the lighthouse.

Swinging the boat round, Chaz headed straight to the shore. It bounced around erratically as it crashed over the breaking waves.

'Brace yourselves,' Chaz shouted as the boat hit the beach with a jolt.

As soon as they killed the noisy engines, the whomp of the helicopter blades took their place, kicking them into action. Fergus and Chaz jumped down while Danny threw the heavy money bags to them. Chaz took three and set off across the sand with a determined march. Fergus followed with two bags over his shoulders and the collapsible ladder in his hand. Finally Danny followed with the last money bag and Smudge's dive bag over his shoulder, and Chaz's toolbox. Trudging relentlessly through the sand, they reached the end of Beach Road with shoulders aching and leg muscles burning. Behind them, the helicopter's search-light engulfed the stolen lifeboat. Popping the boot, they dumped in the toolbox, ladder and as many bags as they could fit in and still shut it. Fergus got in the back of the car, pulling as Chaz shoved the remaining bags in around him. Moving from the lifeboat, the helicopter started sweeping its searchlight towards the road. Chaz and Danny jumped in the front, both slamming the doors shut seconds before the searchlight illuminated them from above.

'Keep in, they'll move off in a minute,' Danny said, as all three of them leaned as far into the centre of the car as possible.

The piercing circle of light and the whomp of rotor blades seemed to hang over them for an eternity. Just as Danny thought the game was up and the police would come charging down the road with sirens blaring to arrest them, the helicopter moved off up the road. Breathing a sigh of relief, the three of them sat tight. The helicopter flew over the main road before banking left, circling over the lighthouse before returning to the beach.

'Right, let's get out of here before we're knee-deep in police,' said Danny starting the car up and moving slowly up Beach Road with the lights off.

'What are we going to do now?' said Fergus, fighting his way between the money bags.

'We've just got to leave a calling card for our friends, then we're off for some sleep. I booked a hotel about a half hour away in Wroxham,' said Danny. He turned onto the main road and flicked the headlights on, driving to the speed limit as they headed back towards Sea Palling.

A couple of minutes later two police cars raced past them on the other side of the road, their lights flashing and sirens wailing as they headed for the stolen lifeboat.

CHAPTER 24

Slade was up early after a bad night's sleep. Smith's friends bothered him. He knew their type, the way they talked, the way they moved; confident, trained, hard men. Ex-servicemen like him, and if they were like him, they wouldn't give up on their friend. He'd have to round everyone up and find them and deal with them quickly before they could cause any more trouble. He drained his coffee cup and was just about to organise the troops when he saw Barney return from the village in the pickup truck. He got out with the shopping from the local Spar and entered the kitchen.

'Alright, guv? You want to see the commotion going on in the village. There's police everywhere. Some arseholes nicked the lifeboat last night and took it for a joyride. The guy in the shop reckons it's beached up at Happisburgh,' said Barney, shaking his head as he put the milk in the fridge.

'Shit, the money, they got the money last night. Get the men up, Barney, get them up NOW,' shouted Slade, picking his gun up off the kitchen table and sliding it into his shoulder holster.

'They can't have, guv, you'd have to be crazy to dive that site at night.'

'You better hope your right. Just get everyone up and ready. I want Smith's friends found,' Slade growled heading out into the courtyard, slamming the door behind him as he went.

Des and Allen were the first ones out, moving over to Slade, who was already in the Mercedes waiting to go.

'Des with me. Allen, you get everyone else out looking for Smith's friends. If you spot them, call me immediately,' Slade said, roaring off the second Des shut the door.

'Where are we going?' Des said, putting his seatbelt on.

'To check out the chalet, see if they've been back there. You got your gun?'

'Yep,' said Des, opening his jacket to expose a Glock handgun holstered under each arm.

They drove along the coast road in silence. Slade's mind was going at a hundred miles an hour. Could they have got the money at night? What was he going to tell the lord and Sir John if they had, and more importantly what would the Dutchman do if he found out his money was gone? When Smudge's cabin came into view, Slade slowed down. Des slid a Glock out of its holster, keeping it low on his lap as he lowered the window, just in case. They got within fifty metres and could see the drive was empty. As they slowed to the front, the place looked deserted, but something fixed to the door caught their eye. With guns down by their sides, the two of them got out, scanning around for prying eyes as they walked cautiously to the front door. Pinned to the centre by a razor-sharp diver's knife was a wad of twenties and a note. Slade worked the knife up and down to release it, then tossed the twenties to Des while he read the note.

You want the money, call me at 6 p.m., and I want to talk to Smith.

There was a mobile number on the bottom of the note and nothing else.

'Fuck,' Slade shouted, thumping the diver's knife deep into the door in anger.

'You're going to have to tell Lord Bartholomew, boss. In a couple of hours Lars is going to know his money is missing. That crazy fucking Dutchman is going to hit the roof,' said Des, sliding the Glock back into its holster.

'I know. So are the lord and Sir John. They've got the clients for the hunt arriving tomorrow. We need to sort these bastards out, they're only two men for Christ's sake,' said Slade getting back into the car.

'What about Metcalf? He's the bloody Chief of Police, get the lord to put pressure on him to find them. It's about time that creep earned his cut,' said Des, getting back into the passenger seat.

'Well, there's no point putting it off. Let's go and see the lord.'

Spinning the car around violently on the shingle drive, Slade showered the chalet with stones before powering off down the coast road.

CHAPTER 25

Barty came down the huge oak staircase that worked its way around the large square reception area. Timms moved gracefully in from the library and stood next to one of the tall, studded, oak front doors. The second Barty's foot hit the stone floor, Timms opened the door for him, standing up straight to one side. Barty didn't acknowledge Timms, he just marched straight out, down the stone steps and carried on across the drive. He stood at the top of the small slope that ran down to a large front lawn, complete with a manicured cricket pitch in the centre. Checking his watch, Barty shielded his eyes from the morning sun and squinted into the sky. A couple of minutes later, the distinctive whomp of helicopter blades faintly filled the air. The noise grew and a black dot became visible on the horizon, growing in size until the helicopter circled overhead before dropping gently down onto the grass. The door opened and Sir John Riddlesworth got out, walking towards Barty with his head down until he was away from the spinning blades.

'Glorious morning, Barty, old man,' said Sir John, climbing the slope before shaking Barty's hand.

'Isn't it just, John? Good flight?'

'Very good, thank you,' Sir John said, looking back at his pilot struggling with his flight case and a large rifle case.

'New toy, John?'

'Oh yes, I've brought a new Benelli Lupo for the hunt tomorrow. I must confess, I'm rather excited to use it,' said Sir John, giving his friend a slap on the back as the two walked back towards the house.

The helicopter's blades wound to a halt, allowing Barty and Sir John's ears to pick up the sound of an engine and crunching gravel as a car approached up the long, treelined drive. They stood at the base of the steps to the house, turning in unison to face Slade and Des as they pulled to a stop in front of them.

'Vincent, Desmond, I wasn't expecting to see you this morning. To what do I owe the pleasure?' said Barty, eyeing them up and down.

'We've got trouble,' Slade said, with a deadpan look.

'Define trouble.'

'Smith's two friends didn't go home like Metcalf said. They broke into the barn last night and got the location of the dive site. After stealing a lifeboat, they got the money and now want to trade it for Smith,' said Slade, handing Danny's note over to Barty.

'What? This is a bloody disaster. We'll have to cancel the hunt, and what are we going to do about Lars?' said Barty, his face dropping as he read it.

'Hold on, Barty, perhaps we could turn this to our advantage. Kill two birds with one stone and all that,' said Sir John, a tight-lipped smile creeping up in the corners of his mouth.

'Please enlighten me, John, because I fail to see how any of this can be anything but catastrophic.'

'Slade, phone this eh. Who did Metcalf say they were?'

'Daniel Pearson and Fergus McKinsey,' answered Slade.

'Right, phone Pearson, let him talk to Smith and arrange the trade for tomorrow night at the clearing in the woods. We're going to give the Sport of Kings clients an added bonus. We get our money for Lars back, and Smith and his friends can spice up the hunt,' said Sir John with a certain amount of smugness.

'Mmm, I like it, John. Bloody genius, old boy,' said Barty, suddenly looking a lot more cheerful.

'They look very handy, ex-servicemen, probably special ops, SAS like Smith. I wouldn't underestimate them.'

'Nonsense, Slade. It'll just add a little more excitement. We'll hunt them down and put a bullet in their heads like we always do. Anyway, if they get close to the boundary, we've got you and your men to take care of them. After all, that is what we pay you for, isn't it?' said Sir John, looking down his nose at Slade.

'Yes, Sir,' Slade said, holding his dislike for the two men back.

After an awkward silence, Slade and Des got back in the car and headed away down the long drive.

'I'd better call the Dutchman and tell him there's a delay with the money,' said Barty, showing Sir John inside.

They moved into the lounge closely followed by Timms.

'Would sirs like some tea or coffee?'

'Tea for two please, Timms,' Barty said after a nod from Sir John.

'Very good, sir.'

They waited for Timms to leave the room before Barty made his call.

'Smythe, this is an unexpected surprise,' came Lars's perfect English with just a hint of a Dutch accent.

'Lord Harrington-Smythe, if you don't mind. One must never forget one's standing,' said Barty, a little annoyed.

'Forgive me, where are my manners? Lord Harrington-Smythe,' Lars replied, still calm and pleasant.

'Right, yes. Anyway, I'm afraid there's been a minor problem with the payment. No big deal, more of a logistics thing. But there is a delay I'm afraid.'

The line was silent for a while, making Barty nervous. Lars's violent reputation preceded him.

'That is unfortunate, Smythe. I will give you one week, and it will cost you another twenty percent, for the additional expenses. One must never forget one's standing, must one?' Lars said, his voice ice cold as he replied.

'Twenty per— Of course, no problem, Lars,' said Barty, nervously.

'One week,' came Lars's curt response before hanging up without waiting for a reply.

Barty stood looking towards Sir John, feeling a little shaken.

'Well, he took that well,' Sir John said with a smile.

'You can call him next time, that man gives me the creeps.'

'What do you expect, Barty, he's a drug dealer, not an accountant.'

With that, both men let out a raucous laugh.

CHAPTER 26

Danny woke with a start. Before you could blink, he sat bolt upright, covering the room with Bill's gun in his hand. The noise of his phone vibrating on the side confirmed what had stirred him. Dropping the gun on the bed, Danny picked the phone up, frowning at Alice's caller ID. He contemplated letting it ring, but he knew she'd only keep trying.

'Hi, love,' he said, yawning and looking at his watch. *11:25.*

'Hiya, am I keeping you up?' said Alice, bright and cheery as always.

'Sorry, Chaz turned up last night and it turned into a bit of a late one,' Danny said, avoiding the nitty-gritty details.

'Oh good, so you've found Smudge?'

'Eh, not exactly. But we have a good idea where he is. We'll have him back soon,' said Danny, trying to sound as if it was a mere formality.

'Ok, so you'll be home soon?'

'Yeah, a couple of days tops.'

'Well, give me a ring when you're on your way, ok? Have fun with the boys. Love you,' she said cheerily.

'Will do, love you too,' Danny said, hanging up and placing the phone down next to a new pay-as-you-go mobile still in its box. He'd picked it up yesterday, ready for Slade to call him to arrange the exchange. He hadn't turned it on yet, in case detectives Taylor and Pilkington traced the number he'd left on the note.

Now he was awake, Danny showered and dressed. His stomach groaned, so he went to raise the others. Using a knock he used to use back when they were a team in the SAS, he only waited a few seconds before Fergus pulled the door open, walking back into the room in his underpants, looking for his jeans.

'You hungry, Ferg?'

'Starving, mate,'

'Alright, I'll give Chaz a knock and meet you in the restaurant,' said Danny, letting the door swing shut on the vision of Fergus's arse crack peeking over the top of his pants, as he pulled his jeans up.

Danny smiled to himself as he walked down the corridor to Chaz's room. Apart from the trouble with Smudge, it was great to be back with his brothers in arms. He repeated the familiar knock on Chaz's hotel room door, barely finishing before it opened. Chaz stood ready to go with a big grin on his face.

'Are we eating, because my stomach thinks my throat's been cut.'

'Yeah, come on, you can eat what you like. It's on Vincent Slade,' Danny said, pulling a wad of twenty-pound notes from his pocket.

'Now you're talking, lead the way, my man,' said Chaz, following him down the corridor.

They took a table on the far side of the restaurant with

views across the terrace to the river and its boats full of day-trippers, but they didn't take the table to sight see; it gave them the longest view across the room to the entrance and had an exit to the terrace and car park behind them, just in case they needed a rapid exit. Fergus joined them just as a pleasant young waitress brought menus to their table. They ordered beers and food and waited until both had arrived before conversation moved to the more pressing matters.

'So what's the plan, boss?' Chaz said, through a mouthful of steak.

'First, we need to talk to Smudge, make sure he's ok,' Danny said.

'And if he's not ok?' said Fergus gloomily.

'We'll cross that bridge when we come to it. For now, we have to believe he's ok,' Danny said, shooting Fergus a look for thinking the worst.

'Ok, ok, Smudge is fine, what about the exchange?'

'Plan for the worst, hope for the best, as always. We have one advantage: they don't know about Chaz,' said Danny raising his pint glass to Chaz.

'That's a first, Chaz, you being described as an advantage,' said Fergus, chuckling.

'Better than being described as a useless waste of space, Ferg,' came Chaz's grinning reply.

'Alright, knock it off, you clowns. Chaz, you got enough stuff on your van to knock us up a few surprises?'

'Eh, yeah, plastic explosive, detonators, timers and a set of ten multi-channel walkie talkies. Should be enough to scare the living shit out of anyone.'

'Good, plus we have one gun. Let's hope we don't have to use them,' Danny said, draining his glass and shaking it to the others as he got up.

'Yeah, same again,' said Fergus.

'Go on then, just one. If we do a little shopping, I can make a few special toys,' Chaz said as Danny and Fergus looked at him with raised eyebrows.

'Just the one it is then,' said Danny, heading for the bar.

CHAPTER 27

Tearing along the farm track through the woods, Slade burst into the courtyard in the Merc, skidding it to a halt in front of the hay barn. He got out and checked his watch.

5:50 p.m., almost time to call that bastard.

'Alright, guv?' said Craig, looking up the stairs as the Portakabin slid back.

'Is he ready?' Slade replied gruffly, his mood not improved since his morning meeting with the toffs.

'Yeah, Allen's cuffed him to the wall. The bastard tried to bite his other ear off,' said Craig, letting Slade past before following him back down into the basement.

'When I get out of here, I'm going to rip your fucking bollocks off and shove them down your throat,' came Smudge's shouts from the cell.

'If you want to get out of here, shut it,' growled Slade, walking into the cell. 'I'm going to call your friend, you say you're alright, then we arrange a trade, that's all. Got it?' said Slade, his eyes angrily focused on Smudge who stopped shouting and nodded, defiantly holding Slade's stare as he dialled.

'Let me talk to Smith,' came Danny's voice down the phone.

Slade stepped in and held the phone to Smudge's ear.

'Danny?'

'Yeah, you alright, buddy?' Danny asked, glad to hear Smudge's voice.

'Yeah, they're a bunch of pussies. I don't know what you've done, but they're really pissed off about something,' Smudge said before Slade whipped the phone away and walked out the cell door.

'Ok, you've spoken to him. Tomorrow night, 8:00 p.m., I'll send the address to your phone. We do the exchange, and you fuck off out of our business, got it?' Slade said, his voice hard, non-negotiable.

'Tomorrow at 8:00 p.m.,' Danny grunted back.

Slade hung up and headed up the stairs. Back in the cell Smudge strained against his cuffed wrists secured through a fixed ring in the wall. He looked up as Allen moved in front of him.

'How's the ear, you ugly bastard?' said Smudge taunting Allen, grinning at his bandaged ear.

'I'll wipe the fucking grin off your face,' Allen said, drawing his fist back and powering it towards Smudge's head.

His actions were slow, giving Smudge time to thrust the hard bone of his forehead forward, headbutting Allen's fist with a bone crunching crack. Allen howled in pain, cradling his damaged fist in his other hand. He stared hatefully at Smudge before scooting out, slamming the cell door shut behind him. A few seconds later Barney opened it with Craig standing a few feet behind him, a Beretta 92 handgun held in his hand.

'No fucking about, Smith,' Barney said, moving behind Smudge with the key to his cuffs.

Craig stayed near the door, his gun pointed at the ground but his face telling Smudge he wasn't afraid to use it. Smudge stayed motionless while Barney unlocked him. He rubbed his freed wrists as Barney and Craig exited the cell, locking the door behind them.

'Tomorrow night at eight,' Smudge whispered to himself, lying down on the hard bed and staring at the ceiling.

CHAPTER 28

The next morning, Barty and Sir John were sitting in the dining room, having just finished a breakfast of smoked salmon and scrambled eggs. Timms entered the room silently, as always. He cleared the empty plates onto a silver tray, never getting so much as a crumb on his immaculate black suit. Barty and Sir John continued talking as if he was invisible, as usual. Their conversation only got interrupted by the roar of a silver Maserati speeding up the drive, a cloud of dust kicked up by its extra wide low-profile tyres.

'Here comes Dickie, keen as ever,' said Barty, getting up from the table.

'Yes, he looks bloody ridiculous in that car. Wait until you see him trying to get out of it, it's hilarious,' said Sir John, following Barty out the front door.

The two of them stood on the top step smirking as they watched Richard Cain push the car door wide open. He stuck one leg out before attempting to pull his chubby body out of the car by shuffling sideways. He eventually stood, shutting the car door with a huff and puff.

'Morning, chaps. She's a beauty, isn't she?' he said, grinning through rosy red cheeks.

'A magnificent beast, Dickie old boy,' Barty said, laughing at Richard's expense. The joke went over Richard's head as usual.

He opened the boot and pulled out a leather Louis Vuitton weekend bag and a T-shaped black case.

'Going for the old crossbow again, Dickie, interesting,' said Sir John, a glint of excitement flashing across his eyes.

'Makes the hunt more interesting. Remember last year? Three arrows in him and he was still going. Are the others here yet?' Richard said through a deep belly laugh.

'No, you're the first. I've put you in the Queen Victoria suite as usual,' said Barty as Timms passed them light-footed down the steps to Richard's side.

'May I take your bags, sir?'

'Yes, thank you, Timms,' said Richard, leaving them where they were and walking away towards the mansion.

Barty's phone started ringing. He frowned when he looked at it. 'Hold on a second, Peter,' he said, putting his hand over the phone. 'You and Dickie go through to the drawing room, I'll be with you in a minute.' He waited until they were inside before continuing his conversation. 'Have you found them?'

'Yes, Barty, they're in a hotel in Wroxham, do you want me to arrest them?'

'No, Peter. I have other plans for Mr Pearson and Mr McKinsey. They are going to be guests of honour at this year's hunt,' said Barty, with an air of superiority.

'And the woman, do I still get the woman?' said Chief of Police Peter Metcalf, a hint of nervousness in his voice.

'You don't deserve it, you were supposed to warn them off,' said Barty, leaving a pause knowing it would drive Metcalf mad. 'As soon as they're in, make sure your men close the coast road, an accident or something will suffice until the hunt is over. Then you can have your prize.'

'Yes, Barty, thank you, I'll make sure it's done.'

Whining little prick.

Barty was just about to go back inside when the sight of a Bentley coming up the drive stopped him. It pulled up beside Richard's Maserati and a middle-aged Japanese man got out.

'Mr Nakatomi, how wonderful to see you again.'

'Lord Bartholomew, it is a great pleasure to be back on the Sport of Kings hunt,' he said standing upright and giving a sharp nod to Barty.

Barty returned the gesture, while the ever reliable Timms appeared to take Kata Nakatomi's bags.

'No, not those,' said Kata, grabbing Timms' arm in a lightning move as he went to pick up an ancient sheathed samurai sword. 'Nobody touches that but me.'

'Very good, sir,' said Timms, unshaken.

'You're in the King Edward suite, Kata. Please get yourself settled and join us in the drawing room when you are ready. I have an unexpected bonus regarding this year's hunt that I'm dying to tell you about,' said Barty, taking full credit for Sir John's idea.

'That sounds very intriguing, I will join you momentarily,' replied Kata, picking up the sword and its shorter twin before following Timms inside.

Just four more to arrive. This is going to be the best hunt yet.

CHAPTER 29

Parked on a patch of land used as an unofficial car park for ramblers and dog walkers, Danny sat on top of the dunes looking out over the sea. Chaz was in the back of his van behind him. He'd been working away for the last couple of hours, only pausing occasionally when the odd curious rambler walked by. Danny turned as the hacksawing from Chaz's van stopped. The sound of a noisy diesel engine announced the approach of a vehicle. A dented, beaten-up, old Ford Transit van bumped into the car park. It pulled alongside Danny's BMW M4 and stopped. When the trailing cloud of diesel smoke cleared, the door opened with a creak and Fergus got out, a big grin on his face.

'Told you, you should have got the wheels,' said Chaz, turning back into his van shaking his head.

'She's sound, mate, don't you worry about that,' Fergus shouted after him.

'Where did you get it from, Ferg?' Danny asked.

'A gypsy site near Norwich. Two grand of drug dealers' money and no questions asked.'

'Good job, let's get it loaded up. It's nearly time to go,' Danny said, checking his watch.

With the money bags in the van, Danny gave Chaz's van a bang on the side.

'You ready, Chaz?'

The side door slid open and Chaz came out with a rucksack and a couple of taped-up bundles the size of a kid's lunchbox.

'Yep, let's have a quick run through,' Chaz said, placing the rucksack down in the back of the Transit. He undid it and pulled out some walkie talkies, giving one each to Danny and Fergus.

'We talk on Channel 9, ok?'

'Yep, got it,' said Danny.

'Now, if the shit hits the fan,' Chaz said, fetching a small plastic box with a doorbell button attached to the front. 'This is for the money. There's enough plastic in the bags to take out a tank, so make sure you're well clear when you hit the button.'

Danny took it and tucked it into his jacket pocket.

'Next there's three of these, throw them, stick them to something, whatever you want. Just flick the switch and you've got around ten second before boom,' Chaz said, handing over three tennis ball-sized lumps of sticky plastic explosive with a detonator and small switch attached to them.

'About ten seconds, that's a bit vague isn't it, Chaz?' said Fergus, taking the ball off him carefully.

'I had to make them out of egg timers from Poundland. What do you want, a guarantee?'

'They're great, top job, Chaz. What about the big ones?' said Danny, pointing to the square bundles.

'Homemade Claymore mines. They're a bit crude, but it's the best I could do at short notice. It'll cut a man to shreds if he gets close enough and will slow 'em down up to twenty metres or so.'

'How do you fire it?' said Danny, picking one up.

'Point the curved side towards the enemy, run the wires out from each corner and wind them round something, then Bob's your uncle, bad guy trips it and a thousand nails and screws blast out the front,' said Chaz, smiling proudly at his creations.

'Outstanding, mate, let's hope we don't need to use them. If it all turns to shit, this is the RV point. I'll leave the keys tucked behind the front wheel. Whoever's left gets in and gets out fast,' said Danny, his face hard as he looked from Fergus to Chaz. They both gave a short nod of agreement, their returning looks as hard and serious as Danny's.

'Ok, forty minutes until we get Smudge back.'

CHAPTER 30

'Gentlemen, the time is upon us. Remember, in addition to your individual choice of prey, there will be two very rare breeds loose in the hunting area. I'm offering free entry to next year's Sport of Kings event, for whoever makes the kill. Now, the vehicles are outside to take you to the start of the fifth annual Sport of Kings hunt. Please keep the glasses we have provided on at all times; we have coated your jackets in a special fluorescent dye that can only be seen through the glasses. This is to prevent any unfortunate accidents in the field,' said Barty, gesturing for the eight men in different camouflaged outfits to head out to the cars. He raised an eyebrow as Kata Nakatomi went past in his full Hitatare samurai outfit. He had the long and short swords attached around the waist, and an antique crossbow slung across his back.

Last out was Sir John in a full one-piece camouflaged hunting suit with his new Benelli Lupo hunting rifle hanging over his shoulder.

'Wish me luck, Barty old boy,' he said, an excited look on his face.

'I rather think it's your prey that needs the luck. Enjoy yourself, John,' Barty said, slapping Sir John on the shoulder as he went outside.

'I will, Barty. And you enjoy the show,' said Sir John, crunching across the gravel before getting in a waiting car.

Lord Bartholomew watched them turn and head off on their three-mile journey, not along the drive but off down a farm track behind the mansion, heading to the centre of the hunting ground. He turned to look at the last glimpse of the sun setting over the front lawn, before shutting the front door and heading down the hall to his library.

'Can I get you anything, sir?' said Timms as Barty passed him near the rear staircase.

'No, Timms, I'm fine. I'll be in my study. I don't want to be disturbed.'

'Very good, sir,' said Timms, moving quietly away.

Barty walked into the library. He ran his fingers along the bookshelf, clicking a small hidden latch. A section of the bookshelf popped forward an inch to reveal a hidden door. Pulling it open, he stepped through into a small room with a computer and three large monitors siting on a desk in a semicircle. Pulling the hidden door shut, Barty took a seat and turned the monitors on. They came alive with thirty-five camera feeds spread across the hunting ground and hay barn with its underground cells. Sliding a headset on, Barty pressed a button on the keyboard.

'Slade, are we all set?'

'Yes, sir. We've dropped the clients off at the starting point. I'm at the rendezvous point now,' said Slade over the sound of the Mercedes.

'And our contestants?'

'All ready for release,' said Slade, with no emotion in his voice.

'Excellent, keep me informed,' said Barty.

'Yes, sir.'

Barty didn't like to hunt himself; he got his buzz from the admiration of his select clients and the large sums of money they were prepared to pay to hunt the ultimate prey. The drugs business was Sir John's idea. Coming from old money gave them status, but the cost of maintaining their ancestors' lavish lifestyles and the upkeep of their ancestral homes was enormous. You either found a way to finance it, or spiral ever downwards until you were no more than a commoner with a title. The thought sent shivers down Barty's spine. The sight of Chief of Police Metcalf's car pulling up at the hay barn brought his focus back to the monitors. Barty picked up the office phone and pressed an extension button.

'Yes, sir?' came Craig's voice.

'Craig, Mr Metcalf has just pulled up. Do show him into the theatre with the women.'

'Yes, sir.'

'Oh and Craig, make sure the cameras are recording. You never know when you might need a little bargaining chip over the Chief of Police,' Barty said with a sarcastic snigger.

'I'll make sure it's on, sir,' said Craig, hanging up the phone.

Craig hit the switch on the wall at the bottom of the stairs. He looked up and watched the Portakabin slide smoothly back to expose Metcalf standing at the top of the stairs, a leather bag by his side. He walked down nervously, his eyes darting around the cellar as if he was about to get caught out at any moment.

'This way,' Craig said, hitting the button again to slide

the Portakabin back into place over the entrance to the stairs.

He walked across to the cell set out like an operating theatre.

'Wait, sorry, no, I have to change first,' said Metcalf, physically shaking as he spoke.

'Eh, ok, the room at the end is empty, you can use that,' said Craig, suitably unimpressed by Metcalf.

Barty watched Metcalf enter the empty room then turned his attention to the Sport of Kings hunters sitting on quad bikes, patiently waiting a little way from the clearing. His eyes sparkled with excitement when he spotted Danny's Transit van on a perimeter camera turning off the coast road and bumping its way down the farm track. Out of the corner of his eye, he spotted Metcalf coming out of the room in full surgical scrubs and face mask.

Sick bastard, I pity that poor girl.

His pity only lasted a fleeting second before he turned his attention back to the clearing and the approaching van. It appeared as though the Transit had stopped on the track, although it was difficult to see as it was at the furthest point between two cameras. Barty was about to contact Slade when the Transit started to move again. Dismissing it, Barty leaned in and watched eagerly.

CHAPTER 31

The closer the beaten-up Transit van got to the destination, the more their mood changed. The banter died down and the professionally trained soldier kicked back in. They'd checked the texted location on Google Earth. The remoteness was a major concern, but having an unknown extra man covering their backs gave them an edge if the deal went sour. Quiet, serious and in tune, the years fell away, the three of them instantly taken back to their SAS days, and the mission was a go. Danny turned at the *Farm Traffic Only* sign as instructed. He bounced along the farm track for a hundred metres until it left the meadow. As the track was swallowed up between the woods, the last of the daylight disappeared and Danny hit the lights. Another hundred metres in, Danny pulled to a stop. The side door opened and Chaz jumped out, a rucksack hooked over his shoulder.

'See you on the other side,' he said, sliding the door shut and heading off into the trees. He vanished into the shadows a couple of seconds later.

'Let's get this done,' said Danny, crunching the old heap into gear and continuing along the farm track.

'Amen to that, brother,' said Fergus, sitting forward as he continually checked the treeline, the Glock handgun firmly in his grip by his side with the safety off.

'Here we go, the clearing's up ahead,' said Danny, keeping the speed low to give Chaz as much time as possible to get into position.

They broke the treeline and pulled into a circular meadow. On the far side, next to a large metal shipping container, sat Slade's Mercedes, facing them with its lights on full beam, their glare making it impossible to see who was behind them.

Danny stopped short on his side of the meadow, his lights also on full.

'Gotcha,' Danny said, opening the door and stepping out.

'Roger that,' said Fergus, opening the passenger door. He stood half-in and half-out of the van, the Glock held just out of sight behind the passenger door.

Slade walked around the Mercedes and stood in front of the bright lights, making him visible only as a silhouette.

'Have you got the money?'

'Where's Smith?' Danny yelled back.

Slade waved his hands to the darkness behind him. A second later two men moved into the light by Slade's side. One was limping slightly, but even with the bright light beaming past the figures, Danny recognised Smudge's outline. The silhouette beside Smudge had a gun pointed at his head. Sliding the side door of the van open, Danny grabbed two of the money bags and carried them along the track until he was halfway between the two vehicles. He dumped them down and backed away to get the others. With their eyes locked on each other, Slade walked to the bags. He crouched down and unzipped one. Taking out a plastic-sealed bundle of money, he held it up into the headlight beam. Satisfied, Slade threw it back in and zipped it up. Standing upright, Slade looked at Danny standing in front of the van, straining under the weight of the four remaining money bags. He stuck his hand up and waved Barney forward. Prodding Smudge to move, Barney walked behind him as he limped from the knife wound in his leg. With his hands tied behind his back and a gag tied around his mouth, Smudge moved towards the money bags. Danny mirrored him, moving towards the centre with the heavy bags until they all came to a stop. His face like granite, Danny stared intensely at Slade, waiting for the next move. Without breaking eye contact, Slade signalled the exchange. Barney prodded Smudge in the back, and he limped across to Danny's side of the money.

'Keep going to the van,' Danny whispered to Smudge. He waited for him to pass before dumping the bags down and walking slowly backwards, away from Slade's hateful stare.

Fergus didn't waste any time untying or taking the gag off Smudge; he hoisted him into the passenger seat and moved round to the driver's side. Ignoring Smudge's mumbled protests, Fergus started the van ready for a hasty retreat.

'Step on it, Ferg,' said Danny, hopping in and slamming the passenger door.

'I'm on it,' said Fergus, spinning around on the slippery grass with the van on full lock.

'Good to see you, Smudge,' Danny said, untying Smudge's hands while he continued to mumble frantically.

The minute his hands were free Smudge ripped off the gag.

'It's a trap, they're planning to hunt us down and k—'

Smudge said panicking, he was interrupted before he finished by a burst of automatic fire from the trees.

The tyres blew out and shredded, leaving Fergus fighting with the wheel, eventually crashing into the trees on the opposite side of the track to the gunfire.

'Fuckers, I'll light the bastards up,' Danny said, hitting the detonator switch in his pocket.

Back at the money, Slade had moved away to the shipping container, leaving Barney to load the money into the Merc. He'd just lifted the first two bags by the handles when they exploded in a huge fireball. The blast severed Barney's arms at the elbows and engulfed him in flames. As Slade's men jumped back shocked, Barney staggered a few paces before collapsing on his front, his screams fading to a gurgle before dying away.

'Go, go, go, into the trees,' Danny said, pulling Smudge out with him.

Fishing one of Chaz's makeshift hand grenades out of his pocket, Danny flicked the switch and hurled it across the road toward the automatic fire. A boom and a gut-wrenching scream echoed from the darkness behind them as they disappeared into the woods.

'You there, Chaz?' Danny said, talking into the walkie talkie.

'Yep, twenty-five metres in, on your three o'clock,' said Chaz, his voice calm and relaxed.

'Roger that. What's up with the leg, Smudge?' Danny said, taking Smudge's arm around his shoulder to support him.

'Bloody Slade stabbed me when he was trying to find out about you. I think the wound's opened up again,' said Smudge, putting his free hand on his thigh to feeling sticky blood.

'Oh great, so that's my fault is it?'

'Yep, sure is. Thanks for coming to get me, mate,' said Smudge, turning serious.

'You'd do the same for me.'

'Nah, I'd fucking leave you,' said Smudge with a wide grin, his teeth and eyes visible in the darkness.

'Tosser.'

CHAPTER 32

Slade watched Barney drop through the flaming shreds of twenty-pound notes floating upward from the burning canvas bags, carried on the rising heat of the fire. His face was as dark as his mood, his cold eyes looking to the trees, searching for a sign of Danny and his friends. Turning away, he pulled the container handle and yanked the heavy metal door open.

'Out, come on, everyone out. Run for your freedom. Now!' he shouted, slapping the side of the container with a metallic boom.

A group of scared faces looked back at him from the rear of the container, unsure of what to do, their blank expressions lit by the yellow and orange light from the fire. Slade's face contorted angrily. He levelled his handgun and shot the man at the front three times in rapid succession in the centre of his chest.

'You won't get another chance, now run. Go, head for the woods,' Slade shouted.

Shocked into action, the remaining men jostled out of the container and ran across the meadow, several jumping to one side in horror as they passed Barney's smouldering body.

'What do we do about Barney and the money, guv?' said Des, moving beside Slade.

Slade glared at him without answering. An uncomfortable few seconds passed before he slid his handgun back in its shoulder holster. Tapping the intercom button on his headset, he spoke. 'Allen, start the hunt.'

Walking over to the Mercedes, Slade opened the boot and pulled out a Steyr Mannlicher Pro Hunter rifle.

'I want the big guy, Pearson. No one touches him.'

'Guv, you can't. Sir John will go mad, the clients have paid to hunt them,' Des said, cautiously trying to reason with him.

'They get in my way, they're dead,' he said, heading across the clearing towards the trees without waiting for Des to reply.

'Shit, this is going to get messy,' Des said under his breath as he watched him go.

The sound of quad bikes grew louder from the farm track behind him until the hunters rode into the meadow and lined up facing the trees. Sir John got off and hurried over to Des.

'What the hell's going on?' he said, eyes wide at the burning heap of money and Barney's dead body.

'Smith's buddies, sir, they booby-trapped the money bags and killed Barney. I think they got Gavin up the track with some kind of homemade hand grenade.'

'Good God, and what the hell is this?' Sir John said, spotting the dead man in the container.

'Slade's taken it personally. He took off after Pearson and Smith,' said Des.

'Goddamnit, eh, ok. We carry on as planned. I'll try to catch up with Vincent. You've got the perimeter covered?'

'Yes, Sir, our best men with sniper rifles.'

Sir John turned away from Des without answering. He walked back to the clients, smiling confidently.

'Gentlemen, let the Sport of Kings hunt begin,' he shouted, above the sound of the quad engines.

The six hunters revved the bikes and hurtled across to the other side of the clearing, followed by Sir John. They turned the engines off when they reached the treeline and selected their weapons of choice from the luggage racks behind them. With the glasses Barty had given them in place, their jackets glowed a faint luminescent green. With their weapons loaded, they fanned out and advanced into the trees, disappearing from view one by one.

CHAPTER 33

'What the fuck's going on, Smudge?' Danny whispered. Fergus followed just behind them, covering the rear with one of Chaz's home-made grenades in his hand.

'They've got some sick hunt going on, a bunch of rich dudes paying a fortune to hunt people,' said Smudge, wincing through the pain in his leg.

'Great, as if we don't have enough problems. Where's Chaz got to?'

'By your left foot, could you two make any more fucking noise?'

Danny looked down to see a pair of eyes and teeth appear from the undergrowth. He sat Smudge down and, with Fergus, dropped to the floor next to Chaz and watched the clearing through the gaps in the trees.

'What's been happening?' said Fergus.

'Your man Slade's not taking the loss of his money well, he's just shot someone in that container and now this lot of crazy fuckers are heading this way,' Chaz said, as all three of them watched the hunt prisoners run and scrabble for the trees as quick as they could.

'There's too many of them to help, they'll have to take their own chances. Let's bug out,' said Danny, not liking it but with a handful of grenades and only one handgun between them, there was nothing else he could do.

'Shit, one of them's heading toward my IED,' said Chaz, springing to his feet and sprinting forward. He took ten paces and leaped over his freshly strung tripwire before rugby-tackling one of the terrified prisoners as he crashed through the trees.

'Help, don't kill me!' he screamed, before Chaz thrust a hand over his mouth.

'Whoa, calm down, buddy, I'm on your side. You don't want to go that way, a few more steps and you'd be kissing your arse goodbye. Take five paces that way then turn 90° right, ok? Then run and keep running until you reach the coast road. Got it?' Chaz said, still on top of the man with his hand over his mouth until he nodded slowly. 'Right, good, now go quickly.'

Chaz rolled off him and left him pacing off before turning and running off, instantly swallowed by the darkness. Pacing his way back, Chaz stepped over the wire and joined the others.

'Let's get out of here.'

'Roger that,' Danny said.

'Wait, lads, they're holding a woman. Some sick fucker's going to torture and kill her,' Smudge said, his voice low.

'We can't, we've gotta get out of here, Smudge, we'll let the authorities know later,' Danny said, the sound of approaching quad bikes urging him to get moving.

'It'll be too late. She's pregnant.'

Danny stood looking across the clearing at Slade as he

fetched a hunting rifle out of the Mercedes. After a few seconds that seemed to last forever he looked at Smudge.

'Fuck's sake. Fuck it, where is she?'

'Follow the track on the other side of the clearing for about a mile and you come to a large hay barn, there's a hidden basement. The entrance is under the Portakabin.'

'Danny, you can't, we've gotta go,' said Fergus, helping Smudge up.

'What's the range on these, Chaz?' Danny said, holding up the walkie talkie.

'About five, six miles.'

'Take this and get to the RV point, kill anyone who gets in your way. No time to argue, just go, I'll keep in contact with the walkie talkie,' Danny said, handing the Glock to Chaz.

Taking it, the three of them gave Danny a nod, then turned and headed into the woods. Danny knelt down as he watched them go. Scooping up mud from the forest floor he covered his face and neck before rubbing mud on his jeans. He glanced back at the clearing. He could see Slade heading for the trees. Behind him, the hunters emerged into the meadow on quad bikes. With one of Chaz's grenades in one hand and a diving knife in the other, Danny headed off in the direction of their wrecked van.

CHAPTER 34

Keeping low, Slade entered the treeline. He moved slowly, attuning his ears to sound of the woods. The sound of the quad bikes ceased and apart from the excited whoops of the hunters, the woods were eerily quiet. Far ahead of him in the darkness he could faintly hear movement, several people by the sound of the twigs and foliage snapping and rustling. Picking the pace up with a trained light foot, Slade headed after the sound. He stopped abruptly at the barely visible signs of flattened ferns and foliage where Chaz had dived on one of their prey. With the smouldering pile of money bags behind him, his senses were on high alert. He pulled a torch out of his pocket and ran its beam forward along the ground, stopping at the silver glint where it reflected off a tensioned wire. Tracing it with the light, the beam shone on a home-made explosive device. There was no surprise or fear on Slade's face, he was ex-special forces; the unexpected was the expected. Calm and focused, he stepped carefully over the wire, switched off the torch and continued to track his prey.

Dwayne and Travis Newton were the first two hunters to enter the woods. The fourth-generation Texan oil billionaires in their early-twenties ran ahead of the others, excited and keen to make the first kill. Waving their ridiculously powerful Accuracy International AX50 rifles ahead of them, they charged like elephants after their prey.

Dwayne stopped. He'd kicked through something thin and sharp across his ankle. He moved his head to look down. His eyes never reached the floor. The blast from Chaz's improvised explosive device and its instantaneous release of its contents of nails and screws blew him backwards, pulping and ripping him to pieces as he went. Half-covered by a tree, his brother caught the blast on the left side, ripping his arm off at the shoulder, popping his eyeball as nails and screws tore through the exposed half of his face, killing him instantly as they penetrated and bounced around inside his skull, turning his brain to mush. Shaken, the other hunters froze on the treeline at the explosion. A second later they all turned to Sir John for answers.

'Just some pyrotechnics to enhance your experience. Get hunting, gentlemen, don't let them get away,' shouted Sir John, adding a hearty laugh to reassure them. Inside, his stomach was turning and his mind was going at a hundred miles an hour. He watched them disappear into the trees before looking over to Des, who shrugged back at him.

'What the hell was that?' he said, following wearily behind Des as they headed through the trees towards the source of the explosion. Sweeping his torch light ahead of him, Des came across what was left of the Newton brothers amongst the shredded undergrowth and nail- and screw-studded trees. Moving past them impassively, Des tried to contact Slade on the headset.

'Oh Christ, this is a disaster. How am I going to explain this?' said Sir John, turning and vomiting when Des's torch lit up the charred, shredded remains of Dwayne Newton.

'Slade's still not answering, Sir. Do you want us to stop the hunt?' said Des, pointing his torch at Sir John's pale face.

'Er, what, eh? No, we carry on. Get your men to clear the bodies away quickly. The other guests mustn't know about this or we'll be ruined,' said Sir John, getting his composure back as he stared nervously into the woods.

Fifty yards away, Kata Nakatomi moved silently along the edge of the woods. He emerged next to the crashed Transit and looked to where he'd seen Danny cross over the farm track, doubling back towards the container and the farm track they'd entered the meadow on. The snap of a twig behind him caused him to spin and draw his long samurai sword in one fluid movement. A few metres away, the soft luminescent glow of Richard Cain's jacket flared through the special glasses as he crashed around with his crossbow in his hand. Startled, Richard looked back at Kata's black Hitatare samurai jacket, also sprayed and glowing softly.

After a quick wave of acknowledgement, Richard headed off into the woods. Kata turned, sheathing his sword, and tried to locate Danny. Just when he thought he'd lost him, Kata caught a glimpse as Danny moved behind the container, vanishing into the trees by the farm track. Kata crossed behind the Transit and set off through the trees in pursuit, moving with precise stealthy strides, barely making a sound.

CHAPTER 35

After seeing the money explode and Barney dropping to the floor in a fiery blaze, Barty started to lose his nerve. He stood and paced up and down in front of the monitors, shooting occasional worried glances in their direction. When the cameras caught the explosion in the trees just after the Newton brothers had entered, Barty sat back down, his face draining of colour, with trickles of sweat running down his forehead.

'Slade, come in Slade, where are you? Slade answer me, man,' Barty shouted through his headset.

Why isn't that infernal man answering?

'John, are you there? What the hell's going on?'

'I'm here, Barty. Smith's bloody friends set a booby-trap in the woods. Dwayne and Travis ran straight into it. I'm afraid they're dead,' said Sir John above the sound of an approaching pickup truck.

'What? How are we going to explain two of the richest men in America dying on my property, and where the hell is Slade?' Barty said, his face going from pale to bright red as his frustration grew.

'Calm down, Barty, nobody knows they're here. They have a suite booked at the Dorchester all week. As far as anyone knows, they're seeing the sights of London. Slade's taken off on some bloody revenge quest and isn't answering his headset. To be quite frank, he's probably the best qualified to deal with them anyway. His guys are clearing away the bodies now, everything's back on track,' said Sir John, convincing himself and Barty, while Des and Allen wrapped the Newton brothers in tarpaulins, and put them in the back of the pickup next to the bodies of Barney and Gavin.

'What about the money? Lars only gave us a week,' said Barty, shivering at the thought of letting the Dutchman down.

'Pah, bloody man's full of hot air. I'll tell the shop to put more mix in the cut, we'll double it up and recoup our losses,' said Sir John, his arrogance returning with gusto.

'Ok, but we can't afford any more problems. I knew it was a bad idea bringing ex-military professionals into the hunt,'

'On the contrary, Barty old boy, doesn't this make the Sport of Kings the ultimate hunt of all hunts?'

'Not if half the clients end up dead,' said Barty gruffly.

'It's not been a great start; I'll grant you that. How are they doing out there?'

'Eh, Dickie and his stupid crossbow has managed a kill. Let me see, ah, our Italian friend has got one, and Mr Hinkle is in hot pursuit over on the far end of the woods.'

'You see, Barty, it's all going fine. What about our Japanese samurai, Mr Nakatomi?'

'Hmm, I haven't seen him for a while, let me see,' said

Barty, scanning the monitors to locate him. Movement near the hay barn caught his eye.

What are you doing over there?

He panned the camera around and zoomed in, freezing to the spot at the mud-covered sight of Danny heading towards the barn.

'John, he's at the barn, bloody what's-his-name, Smith's friend, Pearson,' Barty blurted out in a panic.

The radio crackled with static before Slade's voice came over loud and clear. 'I'm on my way. Nobody else touches him. Des, pick me up on the track, now,' Slade said, spinning around in the woods and running for the farm track.

'Yes, guv, I'm on my way,' came Des's voice in response.

CHAPTER 36

Looking out from behind the trees, Danny checked out the front of the barn. An empty black pickup and Metcalf's car sat outside with no one in sight. The massive sliding front doors to the hay barn were open a few feet, letting a beam of light cut its way across the forecourt like a yellow path. He waited a minute or so, not wanting to get caught out in the open like a sitting duck. When no one came, he ran towards the barn in the darkness beside a hedge. Sliding along the outside of the barn to the opening, Danny stood still and listened for noises from within.

Nothing. All quiet.

He ducked his head in and out again, taking in a mental snapshot of the interior. A stacked-up wall of hay bales, a Portakabin, no noise, no people. Fairly confident of not getting his head blown off, Danny took another look then slid inside. He moved over to the Portakabin and started looking for the switch to make it slide back, exposing the stairs to the basement. When nothing presented itself he tried the Portakabin door thinking the switch might be on the inside. There was nothing inside other than a light switch, a sink, kettle and a microwave with some tables and chairs as a makeshift canteen. The hairs on the back of his neck stood up, and a chill ran down his spine. He hadn't heard the approach; it was more of a feeling, a disturbance in the atmosphere behind him. Danny ducked and kicked out hard behind him, the glint of Kata Nakatomi's samurai blade passing overhead, its ultra-sharp blade slicing a tuft of hair off Danny's head before cutting deep into the soft wooden door frame. Danny's foot made contact with Kata's middle, kicking him back into the barn. Kata landed on his back. A split second after he'd fallen, Kata's legs shot back before being thrown forward, flicking him solidly up onto his feet. Kata narrowed his eyes and moved towards Danny in some sort of martial arts ballet, his samurai sword glinting in a figure-of-eight movement so fast he could hardly see it.

Shit, this isn't good.

Danny moved inside the Portakabin, looking for something to defend himself with. He grabbed the kettle in one hand and picked up a chair in the other, holding it up in front of him like a crap lion tamer. Kata moved inside to face him, his legs slightly bent like tensioned springs, the razor-sharp sword pointed at Danny's neck.

Even though he knew it was coming, the speed of Kata's attack was breathtaking. Danny struggled to keep the chair's metal legs blocking Kata's skilful swordsmanship. He jabbed the kettle through an opening, trying to make contact with Kata's head. The sword flicked round before he got there, its blade slicing through the kettle as though it was made of butter, leaving Danny holding little more than a plastic handle. Danny threw the handle in Kata's face. As he did, Kata thrust the sword forward through Danny's jacket, slicing his side before ripping it out of the material, spilling a homemade grenade onto the floor. With the adrenaline flowing through his veins and the blade being so sharp, Danny didn't feel the cut. He hurled the chair at Kata and dropped to pick up the grenade.

One.

He grabbed the metal leg of a table.

Two.

Danny pulled it up in front of himself like a shield.

Three, four.

He jerked back as Kata struck the veneered wooden tabletop, its tip landing inches from Danny's nose.

Five, six.

When Kata pulled the blade free, Danny tucked in behind the vertical table and charged into Kata, pushing him back until he'd sandwiched him between the table and the sink.

Seven, eight.

Popping upright over the table, Danny swung his arm over and slapped Kata hard on the forehead.

Nine.

Pushing away, Danny ran for the door, diving out onto the barn floor. Covering his ears, he looked back to see a puzzled Kata reaching for the sticky grenade attached to his forehead.

Ten.

The deafening blast disintegrated Kata's head like an exploding watermelon. The rest of his body ripped into pieces, blowing the samurai sword out the door to land at Danny's feet, Kata's hand still gripping its handle.

Poundland egg timers… Nice one, Chaz.

He peeled the hand off and picked up the sword as the flaming Portakabin started to roll back. Jumping to his feet, Danny moved to its side and stayed at its corner, matching the speed as it rolled away from the stairs. Looking down, he could see Craig coming up with his gun out in front of him. Spinning around, Danny leaped from above, the samurai sword held in both hands above his head as he powered it down with all his might. It struck Craig on one side of his neck. The ultra-sharp blade cut through bone and muscle, not stopping until it reached his navel. He stayed upright for a couple of seconds, his brain unable to comprehend the devastating assault on his body. He finally fell forward with a low gurgling sound coming from his mouth and a sickening slurp as the sword slid out of the wound.

Dropping the sword on the stairs, Danny picked up Craig's gun and turned, squatting down to see into the basement. He could hear loud music playing from somewhere on the other side, but nobody came running. Sliding the magazine out of the gun, Danny was happy to see it was full. Sliding it back in, he cautiously moved down the stairs, step by step.

CHAPTER 37

Richard Cain had his eyes on two shapes in the distance. One looked to be helping the other, their silhouettes appearing intermittently as the moonlight caught them through the occasional break in the trees. In his mind he was closing on them silently with the stealth of the ultimate hunter. In reality, he crunched and snapped his podgy way through the undergrowth. Breathing heavily, he took cover behind a tree to get his breath back, the shadow of his belly sticking out one way, while his arse stuck out the other.

Come on, Dickie, bag these two and you're bound to beat John in the hunt.

He set off again, swearing as he snagged his trousers on some brambles. Freeing himself, he panicked when he couldn't see his targets and broke into a shuffling run, crashing his way forward until he picked up their silhouettes again. Richard brought up his crossbow, taking aim through its telescopic sight. They were still too far away, disappearing in and out of sight between the trees. He ran some more, gaining ground and a better view on his target.

Using a tree branch to steady his aim, he looked through the sights again. In his magnified view, Richard could see one man being helped by the other, his arm around a shoulder as he limped beside him. Richard moved the crosshairs between the shoulders of the uninjured man. If he took him out first, the other one would be easy prey.

Deep breath, Dickie, clean shot.

A click from behind him broke his concentration. 'I say, go and find your own target. This one's mine,' he said, turning angrily to see the barrel of a gun pointed at his forehead.

'Evening, dickhead,' said Fergus, pulling the trigger.

Picking up Richard's crossbow, Fergus peeled away from the body and melted into the darkness.

'You bag yourself an elephant?' said Chaz when Fergus appeared beside him and Smudge.

'Yeah, big fat fucker at that. How you holding up, Smudge?'

'I've lost a bit of claret, but I'll live. What's with the toy?' said Smudge, looking at the crossbow.

'I thought it was cute, I was going to take it home for the kids,' chuckled Fergus.

'Camera, ten o'clock,' said Smudge, looking up into the trees, causing all three of them to peel away to the right, putting more trees between them and the camera.

They went twenty metres before turning back on their original course. After a short distance, they put Smudge down and tightened the blood-soaked bandage around his leg. Satisfied, they lay on their fronts and crawled another ten metres forward. Smudge rolled painfully on his front and pulled himself along to join them.

'The edge of the treeline,' said Fergus, scanning the moonlit meadow leading up to the coast road through the last few rows of trees.

'Yep, what do you think?' said Chaz.

'Last line of defence, they can't afford for any of us to get out. If I were them, I'd have snipers spaced along the treeline to take anyone out as they make a break for the road.'

'Yeah, that's what I was thinking, left or right?' said Chaz, his teeth showing up as he grinned.

'Left. Here, you take the gun, I'm going to have a go with the kids' toy,' said Fergus, handing over the gun.

'Great, what do I do?' grumbled Smudge.

'Sit tight, you've done enough, it's your fault we're in this mess,' said Chaz, getting up and patting him on the shoulder.

'Oh, thanks, make me feel better why don't you.'

'Just sit tight, we'll be back in a bit,' said Fergus, moving silently off through the trees.

'Just me and you then, Chaz,' said Smudge, turning back to find Chaz had already vanished into the woods. 'Brilliant.'

Moving silently inside the treeline, Chaz scanned the meadow's edge for telltale signs of a bedded-in sniper: camouflaged netting, a barrel sticking out of the undergrowth.

Where are you?

Flattening himself to the ground, Chaz belly-crawled slowly to the edge of the meadow. He leaned back against a tree trunk and craned his neck around to look up and down the treeline. He still couldn't see anything out of the norm. A creak and a scattering of pine needles from above caught his attention. Looking up, it surprised Chaz to see the underside of a wooden platform, the barrel of a rifle just visible as it poked over the edge. Inching himself upright, Chaz moved round the trunk to find a row of wooden blocks screwed into the trunk, forming a ladder up to the platform. Placing the gun in his belt, Chaz pulled a diver's knife from his jacket. Sliding it out of its sheath, he placed it between his teeth and started to climb. Turning his head as he came up through the platform, Chaz froze at the sight of the sniper's leg lying right in front of his eyes. Breathing softly, Chaz carried on moving up the makeshift ladder until he could move his foot over the unsuspecting man lying flat on his front, his attention still focused on the meadow through his rifle sight.

Placing his foot down, Chaz rolled it silently from the tip of his toes to the flat of his sole on the wooden surface. Letting go of the makeshift ladder with one hand, Chaz took the diver's knife out of his mouth. He took his other foot off the wooden rung to place the other side of the sniper, ready to dive forward and plunge the blade into the back of his neck, severing the spinal cord. As his foot rolled on the deck, the board creaked. Alerted, the sniper spun onto his back as Chaz lunged down at him. He caught Chaz's wrist with a shovel-sized hand, stopping the blade inches from his nose.

Being on top, Chaz tried to use all his body weight to drive the knife into the sniper, but the man was fast and strong. He punched Chaz hard in the ribs with his free hand, then tried to roll him off the platform. Chaz shot his arm out and grabbed the branch above him to stop himself falling. Another blow to his ribs left Chaz gasping for breath.

The sniper moved his other hand to Chaz's wrist and started twisting the blade around to point at Chaz. Winded and off balance, Chaz couldn't let go of the branch to grab his gun or he'd fall, and he couldn't stay where he was or this guy would stab him with his own knife.

The sniper knew he had him. A cold grin spread across

his face as he prepared to drive the blade home. Gritting his teeth, he went for the final push.

It never came.

A cracking sound came from the back of his head and the tip of a crossbow bolt burst from one eye, killing him instantly. His body went limp, and he fell to the side, disappearing off the platform. The view of Fergus holding the crossbow with a big grin on his face took the sniper's place.

'Come on, Chaz, stop pissing about with your new mate.'

Chaz dropped the sniper's rifle down to Fergus and climbed back down the ladder.

'Not a bad toy that,' Chaz said, pointing at the crossbow.

'Yeah, I know, the kids are going to love it.'

CHAPTER 38

Back in the mansion, Barty's eyes flicked around the screens, panic setting in. He couldn't get hold of Sir John, Slade wouldn't answer, and he couldn't get hold of any of the men on the perimeter. Added to that, he'd just seen Kata Nakatomi get blown to bits, and Craig hacked nearly in two by Pearson before he descended into the basement.

Oh Christ, Metcalf's down there with the girl.

Grabbing his phone, Barty struggled with the buttons, his shaky fingers struggling to find Metcalf's number.

In the cell-cum-operating theatre, the large, motorised chair had been raised and flattened to form an operating table. Metcalf picked up a bottle of smelling salts and moved to the unconscious woman strapped to the table. A few wafts under her nose and Susan Wimple's eyes flicked open, staring widely at the terrifying sight of Metcalf in full surgical scrubs and a paper mask. She wanted to move, to scream, to escape, but the straps held her tight around her legs, arms and body. Worse still was the strap around her neck and forehead, holding her rigid, forcing her to look at that evil man. She struggled to breathe through the wide gag strapped across her mouth, its plastic ball filling the inside so she couldn't shut or swallow properly.

'Welcome back, my dear. Let's give you a little adrenaline shot, shall we? I wouldn't want you to pass out again and miss out on the main event,' said Metcalf jabbing her in the arm with a syringe before folding the sheet back to expose her naked pregnant belly.

Tears rolled down her cheeks as she quivered, every little movement racking her with pain where he'd removed her left breast and amputated her right hand, both sewn up and bandaged after she'd had passed out. His phone buzzed on the stainless steel instrument trolley as he checked the saline drip. Seeing Lord Bartholomew's caller ID, he grabbed it and answered.

'What? Hang on, Barty, I can't hear you, I'll turn the music down,' he said, putting the phone down and walking to the back of the room to turn down the music volume.

The door open behind him, and Danny slid inside with his gun levelled at Metcalf. His face hardened at the sight of Susan's tortured body and the severed hand laying on the instrument table. His dark eyes narrowed as they looked along the gun sights at the back of Metcalf's head.

Turning round, Metcalf continued his conversation with Barty, his mind focused on the phone call rather than Danny by the door.

'Right, sorry, Barty, what w—'

He froze mid-sentence, fear and confusion displayed in his eyes as he lowered the phone slowly. Barty's metallic voice could still be heard shouting through the phone's tiny speaker as he talked at a hundred miles an hour.

'Eh. This, this is not what it looks like. Look, I'm the Chief of Police, you can't touch me, I'll have y—'

With robotic precision, Danny moved the gun and fired, then moved the gun and fired again, each bullet finding the centre of Metcalf's kneecaps, shattering them as they passed through and destroyed the joints behind. Leaving Metcalf rolling around screaming in agony, Danny moved over to Susan and removed her restraints.

'It's alright, I'm going to get you out of here,' he said, trying not to show his shock at the sight of her removed breast sitting on the tray beside them.

As soon as she was free, she clung to him, shaking uncontrollably, barely able to speak after an eternity gagged.

'Shh, it's ok. Do you think you can stand?' Danny said firmly, looking at her in the eyes, trying to get her to focus on his words.

Eventually she returned his gaze and nodded. 'Yes,' she said hoarsely.

'Good, we need to move,' Danny said looking around until he spotted her clothes folded up on a shelving unit in the corner.

While Metcalf continued to gasp and shriek on the floor, Danny helped her dress, taking care when sliding the stump of her right arm through her jacket as she sat pale and shaking.

'What about him?' she said, strength and clarity coming back into her voice as she looked at Metcalf in disgust.

'Up to you,' Danny said, flipping the gun around to offer her the grip.

'Did they kill my boyfriend?'

'Yes. Sorry, yes they did,' Danny said, watching her eyes tear up again.

She snatched the gun out of his hand and pointed it at Metcalf's chest. His eyes went wide and he started to say something, but she pulled the trigger twice before the words could leave his mouth. The force of the bullets flattened him to the ground, leaving him staring lifelessly at the ceiling as his last breath left his body.

'Ok, it's ok. Now let's get you out of here,' Danny said, easing the gun out of her hand.

Spotting Metcalf's phone on the floor, Danny picked it up and put it to his ear.

'Peter, Peter, watch out, he's there. He's in the bloody basement, I saw him on the camera. Peter?'

Danny took it away from his ear and looked at the ID displaying Lord Bartholomew Harrington-Smythe.

'I'll be seeing you real soon,' he said, moving it back to his mouth, with a look as dark as his mood.

He put the phone in his pocket and turned to the stainless steel tray. Picking up Susan's dismembered hand, Danny placed it in a plastic bag.

'They might be able to sew it back on,' he said, tucking it into her jacket pocket with the best reassuring smile he could muster.

She shook and nodded, partly in shock, partly in understanding, and followed a few steps behind, shuffling on unsteady feet. Danny went ahead to check the basement was clear. Smoke was floating in an eerie waist-high layer and a flickering orange glow emanated from the top of the stairs.

'We've gotta go, now,' Danny said, turning and picking her fragile body up in his arms.

She let out a painful gasp but didn't complain as he ran as fast as he could across the basement and up the stairs. As he emerged into the hay barn, the intense heat crinkled the skin on the back of his neck. The fire in the Portakabin had burnt its way through the roof, its sparks and embers drifting across the gap to the mountain of hay stacked behind it. Half the stack was alight, thermals from the intense heat causing a mini fire tornado, spinning and igniting the hay above it. With the heat and smoke making his head spin, Danny headed out the door into the welcome cool night air. He put Susan down carefully and headed for the vehicles. Metcalf's car was locked, but the pickup was open. Looking in, he let out a sigh of relief at the keys hanging from the ignition. Returning, he helped Susan into the passenger seat before getting in and starting it up.

'Next stop, hospital.'

CHAPTER 39

'Close it down, close everything down!' said Barty, almost screaming down the mic.

'Yes, boss,' came Bill's response.

Standing up, Barty paced up and down his office. More men were dead, and he'd just seen Pearson coming out of the burning barn with the woman in his arms.

'You there, Barty? What's all this about shutting the hunt down, I thought we had things under control?' came Sir John's indignant voice.

'No, we bloody well don't have things under control. It's your fault! Ex-special forces, the ultimate prize, you said. Well, nearly everyone's dead and Pearson's just killed Kata Nakatomi, Craig and Metcalf. Christ knows where his friends have gone.'

'What, they're dead, how? Never mind, I'll round up the clients and come to you. Get the men to take the bodies to the pig barns and dispose of them. We must get rid of everything. The grounds and the farm are all leased to the dummy marine research company, there's nothing to lead back to you or I. Just sit tight, Barty old boy, it'll be alright,' said Sir John, his tone softening as he spoke.

'But he said he was coming for me.'

'Who?'

'Pearson,' Barty said, a tremble in his voice.

'I thought Slade was taking care of him. Where is he?'

CHAPTER 40

After reversing the powerful pickup truck around, Danny shoved it in first and headed for the farm track to the coast road. He'd just bumped down off the concrete courtyard onto the shingle track when the rear window imploded, the bullet exiting with a neat hole through the laminated layers of the front windscreen. In his rear-view mirror Danny could see the other pickup truck sliding sideways onto the courtyard. Slade stood in the back holding onto the roll bar with one hand while he popped off rounds from a handgun from the other.

'Keep as low as you can,' Danny said to Susan, her face contorted with the pain of her injuries, aggravated by the bouncing around on the dirt track.

He had no choice. Danny flattened the accelerator to the floor, the vehicle snaking along the track until its chunky tyres got a grip. He glanced in the wing mirror to see a flash from Slade's gun, the shot blowing the mirror into a million pieces, leaving a shard of broken plastic in its place. Feeling for the only pocket left in his shredded jacket, Danny found the walkie talkie and clicked it on.

'Chaz, you there?'

'Yep, go ahead. Over,' came Chaz's welcome voice over the noise of the revving engine.

'What's your location? Over,' Danny shouted as another bullet ricocheted off the roll bar over the driver's cab.

'We are on the coast road, about a mile from the RV point. Over,' said Chaz.

'I'm on my way, but I'm coming in hot. Over.'

'How many? Over.'

'Two, armed, in a pickup truck. Over,' said Danny, hitting a pothole which sent him ploughing through the verge until he got the vehicle back on the track. Susan groaned in agony beside him.

'Bring them in, I've got a surprise for them. Over and out.'

'Sorry, just hold tight for a little longer,' Danny said, trying to comfort her.

A few seconds later they flew out of the treeline and across the meadow to where the track met the coast road. Barely slowing at all, Danny yanked on the handbrake and slid the pickup sideways onto the road before dropping the brake and pressing the accelerator flat to the floor. Barely thirty metres behind them, Des pulled an identical manoeuvre, with Slade hanging tightly onto the cab's roll bar. Straightening up, Des screamed the pickup in each gear to catch up with them.

Danny got another half a mile down the bendy road before a hail of bullets ripped and ricocheted off the rear corner of his pickup.

Shit, he's going for the tyres.

'Where are you guys? I'm taking a lot of fire here,' Danny shouted down the walkie talkie.

'Keep coming, mate, we can just see you in the distance. Over,' said Chaz.

'You got this, Smudge?' said Fergus, watching Smudge rest the sniper rifle Chaz had taken off the man in the tree on the estate wall for support.

'Yep,' said Smudge, not looking at him as he concentrated through the telescopic sight.

'Your leg's not going to put you off?' said Chaz next to him.

'Nope.'

'He's going to miss,' said Fergus casually.

'Nah, he'll do it,' Chaz replied as if they were talking about the weather.

'Twenty says he misses,' said Fergus.

'Twenty, you're on,' said Chaz sticking his hand out so the two men could shake on it.

'I am fucking here, you know,' grumbled Smudge as he slowed his breathing for the shot.

'Come on, Smudge, any closer and I could hit 'em with my toy crossbow,' Fergus said with a chuckle.

'Fuck off, Ferg,' Smudge mumbled, his body motionless. He stopped breathing mid-way through full exhalation and squeezed the trigger slowly and smoothly.

There was a second's delay as the bullet travelled the half-mile to its target, punching a neat hole through the windscreen then a not-so-neat hole between Des's eyes, blowing the back of his head off before it exited and shattered the window behind him. Before Slade realised what had happened, the pickup truck veered to one side, crashing into the estate wall as it came to an abrupt stop. Thrown forward with immense force, Slade hit the back of the cab with his legs before somersaulting over the top of the vehicle and landing hard in the meadow beyond.

'Ah bollocks,' Fergus said, digging into his pocket.

'Come on, cough it up,' grinned Chaz, taking the twenty off him.

'Still got it. Best shot in the Regiment,' said Smudge, standing upright and waving to Danny as he pulled up beside them.

'Good to see you, boys. Hop in the back and let's get the fuck out of here,' said Danny, leaning across to shout out of Susan's window.

'Roger that,' said Fergus, helping Smudge into the back of the pickup.

All in, they headed off for the RV point. Half a mile behind them, Slade struggled to his feet in the grassy meadow. He watched their taillights fade into the distance before limping back to the crashed pickup. With the screech of bent metal on bent metal, he yanked the driver's door open and heaved Des's body across into the passenger seat. With a lot of revs, the four-wheel drive got enough grip to drag the vehicle out of the wall. It juddered badly as Slade turned it around, then screeched as he drove it back towards the hay barn.

CHAPTER 41

'This is a bloody shambles, Barty, I will be expecting a full refund.'

'I can only apologise, Edward, I'll make it up to you, I promise,' said Barty, as the last of his Sport of Kings clients spun his Porsche around on the gravel and headed off down the long drive, eager to get as far away from Lessingham Hall as possible, and even keener to disassociate himself from Lord Bartholomew Harrington-Smythe and Sir John Riddlesworth.

'Flashy young upstart. If I hadn't given his father a leg up all those years ago, that little shit would be working in McDonald's,' Sir John said indignantly.

The screeching whine of Slade approaching in the damaged pickup stopped Barty from answering. The vehicle appeared from the farm track in a cloud of steam from its fractured radiator. Slade shouldered the door open with a metallic screech and pulled himself out of the gap.

'Did you get him?' said Sir John, his eyes wandering to Des's body slumped in the passenger seat.

'No, he got away with the girl. Where's Metcalf? We're

going to need his help,' Slade said, slamming the door in frustration.

'We're done for, John. Peter's dead, Pearson shot him, we can't pay our way out of this,' said Barty, panicking again.

'Keep calm, Barty, this could work to our advantage,' said Sir John, thinking.

'How, how the hell could this work to our advantage?' said Barty, pacing up and down the drive.

'We get rid of everything, bodies, cars, and destroy the basement, but leave Metcalf's body. Vincent, you fill the boot of his car with drugs and cash. I can get my legal man to draw up a backdated lease agreement for the land with Metcalf's name on it. The publicity will make them want to shut the investigation down quickly — perverted Norfolk Chief of Police deals drugs and tortures young woman. Perfect,' said Sir John, pleased with his own ingenuity.

'Ok, I'll do it, but once we're clear, I want Pearson,' Slade said, his menacing look making it very clear he didn't want to argue about it.

'Get it done and join me at my London estate. When the heat is off, Pearson is all yours,' said Sir John, turning at the sound of a distant helicopter approaching. 'Ready, Barty?'

Timms appeared from the front door with a small carry-on suitcase for Barty and the rifle case and bags Sir John came with.

'Your bags, sirs,' he said, waiting to carry them to the helicopter.

'Thank you, Timms. Remember, when the police arrive, I've been staying at Sir John's residence all week.'

'Very good, sir.'

The helicopter banked round over the house before touching down in the middle of the cricket pitch on Barty's front lawn. Ducking down, Sir John and Barty shielded their eyes against the dust and grit from its downdraft. They climbed in and buckled up, placing the sound-cancelling headphones on their heads.

'Good evening, Frederick, could you take us to the Claymoor estate? As quick as you like, please,' Sir John said over the intercom.

'Very good, Sir,' he replied.

As soon as Timms secured the bags in the small luggage compartment and moved clear, Frederick wound up the blades and pulled the helicopter sharply skywards. As it tipped forward and gained speed, Barty watched Slade climb in the pickup and spin it around on the gravel drive before tearing off towards the barn and farmhouse.

'At some point in the future I think Vincent might become a problem,' he said, the microphone and sound-cancelling technology in the headphones making him sound far away.

'I'm sure you're right, dear boy, and when that moment arrives, we'll get rid of him,' said Sir John with no hint of emotion.

CHAPTER 42

After skidding to a halt by the vehicles, Danny helped Susan into his BMW M4. Her face was pale and he could tell she was in a lot of pain, but she still managed a smile when she was in. He was about to shut the passenger door when she touched his arm.

'Thank you, thank all of you. I owe you my life,' she said, her voice quiet and weak.

'No, you don't owe us anything, but you can do us a favour,' Danny said smiling back.

'I wouldn't get too excited, you've seen him drive, we'll be lucky if we get to the hospital alive,' chuckled Smudge from the back of the car.

Danny walked over to Chaz by his van. 'You off back to Scotland?'

'Yeah, as far as anyone knows, I never left. I'll catch up with you in a couple of weeks when the contract's done,' said Chaz.

The two men embraced and slapped each other on the back.

'Get a room, you tarts,' shouted Fergus from Danny's car.

'I'll catch up with you in a couple of weeks, Ferg,' Chaz said with a nod. Their eye contact shared a bond only men who'd fought together knew.

'Chaz. Thanks for coming back for me, brother,' said Smudge, leaning out of the car window.

'You'd have done the same for me,' Chaz replied, giving him a wink.

They all got in and headed their separate ways, Danny's considerably quicker as he took off for the hospital in the powerful 3-litre twin-turbocharged sports car. Even though the roads were bad, at three in the morning they barely came across another car, and approached the hospital's accident and emergency in no time. Danny pulled up short of the approach road, watching an ambulance as it stopped by the entrance doors.

'Ready?' he said to Susan.

'Yes,' she replied.

He got out and went round to the passenger side. Opening it, he slid his arms under Susan and lifted her out of the car. After a second look, Danny ran as fast as he could with Susan in his arms up the approach road to the back of the ambulance. Climbing in the back, he laid her on the bed and backed out.

'Tell them all about those bastards, ok?' Danny said with a smile.

'Thank you. Now go, get out of here,' she said, wincing with the pain.

Danny turned and ran back towards the car. He wasn't worried about the cameras at the entrance. Still caked in mud from head to toe, his own mother wouldn't recognise him. In the back of the ambulance Susan counted to twenty and started yelling and banging on the side of the ambulance. By the time the medics came running out, Danny had turned the car and disappeared into the night.

'She'll be alright, tough girl that,' said Smudge from the back.

'Yeah, she is. What about you, are you sure you don't need the hospital for your leg?'

'Nah, it'll be alright, a clean bandage and a few beers and it'll be right as rain in a few days.'

'The last few days have been a picnic compared to what Carol's going to do to me when I get back in this state,' said Fergus in the passenger seat.

'There's something in the glove box that might put a smile on her face,' said Danny, grinning through his mud-caked face.

Fergus flicked the glove box open to see three plastic-sealed bricks of twenty-pound notes looking at him.

'Ha ha, fucking hell, you sneaky bastard,' he said, throwing one to Smudge in the back.

'What about Chaz?' said Smudge.

'I put one in the back of his van, he'll have a nice surprise when he gets to work tomorrow,' said Danny, turning onto the A11 and heading for London.

'Nice one. Take me home, my good man,' said Smudge laughing.

'There's just one thing I'd like to do first,' Danny said, his face turning serious.

'Here we go, don't tell me you left your wallet in the woods,' Smudge joked from the back.

'Go on, what is it?' said Fergus, ignoring Smudge.

'A little payback.'

CHAPTER 43

After strange looks from motorists and a security guard that followed their every move, the three of them managed to clean off most of the mud and grime in the motorway services toilets. With tiredness and fatigue and the comedown after the adrenaline of the night's action, Danny, Chaz and Fergus hit KFC and demolished several buckets of chicken and sugary fizzy drinks, the hit from both waking them back up. On the move again, they left the motorway as the sun crept above the horizon, and pulled into a 24-hour Tesco on Ponders End, Enfield. Looking slightly less like a tramp than Danny, and without the blood stains down his leg like Smudge, Fergus went in. He emerged fifteen minutes later with bags full of jogging bottoms, T-shirts and hoodies, and disinfectant and bandages for Smudge's leg.

'What about the glasses and scarves?' Danny said.

'They're in the bottom of the other bag.'

'Ok, great,' said Danny, with a smile.

They stripped off and changed in the car park, not

caring about the strange looks and a couple of wolf whistles from passing shoppers.

'Everything in the bag, boys, I'll burn them later before I dump the weapons in the canal,' Danny said, passing the carrier bag to Smudge.

'Aw, I wanted to keep the crossbow,' Fergus grumbled.

'We get rid of everything, Ferg. Anyone asks, we went up to meet Smudge. Had a couple of days at the chalet, drunk a lot, then came home two days ago. Before the lifeboat theft and the hunt, ok?'

'Yeah, got it. Wait, what lifeboat?' said Smudge.

'I'll tell you later,' said Fergus.

Moving across London before the morning rush hour traffic got heavy, they reached Chelsea just after 7:00 a.m. After a quick tour of a McDonald's drive-through for more coffees, Danny parked the car and sat quietly drinking while studying their target a few buildings down the road.

'How many do you think are in there?' said Smudge, leaning forward to see out between Danny and Fergus in the front.

'Best case, two armed guys guarding the drugs and five or six cutting and bagging the merchandise. Worst case, a room full of armed, pissed off drug dealers,' said Danny, spotting the *Riddlesworth Fish Merchants* refrigerated van coming along the road.

'Fucking walk in the park, mate, let me at 'em,' said Fergus sarcastically.

'You two don't have to come,' said Danny, checking the Glock handgun before slipping it in his hoodie.

'Fuck off, you can't even tie your own shoelaces without us. Besides, Ferg wants one last chance to shoot someone with his toy arrows before you throw it in the river,' sniggered Smudge as he checked the other handgun.

'Alright then, scarves on, hoods up and glasses on, boys.

Let's teach these fuckers a lesson,' said Danny, the demeanour of the three instantly changing: faces hardening and eyes sharp and alert.

The driver had already parked the refrigerated van and entered the shop area at the front of the fish merchants. Danny and Fergus got out of the car first, crossing the road as Smudge limped after them. Pulling the gun from his hoodie pocket, Danny moved inside the door and stepped to one side, making room for Fergus to pass him, covering the shop with his crossbow. The two men in long white coats and white hats behind the counter looked up to see who had entered and froze to the spot.

'On the floor, now. Stay there, keep quiet and you won't get hurt,' said Danny through the scarf across his mouth and nose. With the hood up and sunglasses on, there was virtually no part of him visible to identify.

He and Fergus walked forward, brushing a chain-link fly curtain to one side to enter a preparation room, with its sinks and stainless steel tables and selection of different fish knives hanging along the walls. They didn't look behind them; they knew Smudge would be in the shop by now, watching over the workers and covering their exit. At the back of the prep room was another door. Standing on either side, Fergus nodded to Danny as he stretched across and grabbed the handle.

'One, two, three,' he whispered to Danny, whipping the door open as quickly as he could.

Danny spun into the room, instantly shoving his gun in the face of a thickset guy sitting at a table, a bacon sandwich in one hand and a mug of tea in the other. Unfortunately for him, his gun was sitting on the table in front of him, out of reach. He sensed Fergus's movement behind him, followed by the snap as the crossbow string propelled a bolt forward. Danny turned and saw a man at the far side of the room drop his gun and fall to the floor with a crossbow bolt protruding out of both sides of his shoulder. Throwing the crossbow on the floor, Fergus picked up the gun on the table and moved into the centre of the room, standing between the two drugs-laden rows of tables that ran its length.

'Now keep calm and nobody gets hurt,' he said, eyeing the dozen women dressed in white paper overhauls, latex gloves and face masks.

They dropped the assortment of cocaine and cutting agents and little sealed plastic bags by their weighing scales and backed away with wide, scared eyes. From the little he could see of their faces they were from the Far East, Thailand perhaps, probably trafficked into workhouse slaves. Danny moved up beside Fergus and handed him the other gun while he flicked the rucksack off his back. He reached in and took out Chaz's second homemade bomb, placing it on the table. Fergus stood behind him with a gun outstretched in either direction as he moved his head from one guard to the other, making sure they didn't try anything.

'Ready?' Danny said, untangling the coiled-up wire attached to the explosive device.

'Yep,' said Fergus through the scarf across his mouth.

'Right, everyone out, NOW!' Danny shouted.

Fergus pointed one of the guns up and fired two shots off into the ceiling. The noise was deafening in the small room but had the desired effect, shocking the women into action as they screamed and made for the door. The guard at the end moved slower, holding their gaze with hateful eyes as he moved out, his hand gripping his shoulder with the crossbow bolt still sticking out of it. He was joined at the door by the other guard. They both backed away through the preparation room with Fergus following, guns pointed unwaveringly at their heads. Danny came out last, unwinding the wire as he went.

'Come on, jog on, move,' said Smudge by the shop door, ushering the women past him. He backed out onto the pavement as Fergus came through and waved them off up the road with the gun.

Fergus joined him outside and put a couple of bullets through the refrigerated van's window, causing more screams and the crowd to run down the road in the opposite direction to Danny's car.

'Good job, boys. Now, if you don't mind, I think you might want to move away from the shop front for this one,' said Danny, trailing the wire to one side of the building before giving it a big yank.

The explosion was deafening, followed by the instantaneous blowout of the front windows, showering the refrigerated van and cars in the road in a million glass shards. Danny and the boys walked round and peered in to see the centre of the building engulfed in an orange fireball.

'I should have brought the marshmallows,' Fergus said, chuckling.

'I wouldn't breathe too heavily, mate, you'll be high as a kite for a week,' Smudge said, looking at all the black smoke billowing out from the top of the building.

'Come on, we're done here, let's go home,' said Danny, satisfied.

'That'll teach the fuckers,' said Fergus, as he and Danny walked to the car with Smudge limping closely behind them.

CHAPTER 44

'Shall we play a round this afternoon, Barty?' said Sir John, sitting in the huge drawing room at Claymoor Manor.

'I don't know how you can think of golf after last night,' said Barty, looking pale and tired as he sipped tea from a bone china cup.

'On the contrary, old boy, being out and seen is exactly what we should do, don't you think?'

'Mmm, I suppose so. But I don't think my game will be much good,' said Barty, agreeing reluctantly.

'Excellent, shall we say one o'clock? I'll get Michaels to knock us up a bit of lunch before we go,' said Sir John, seemly undisturbed by the events of the night before.

'I was just thinking about poor old Dickie,' said Barty, gazing into his teacup.

'Yes, dreadful shame, a bloody good barrister as well. He won't be easily replaced.'

'Christ, John, is that all you can think about? He was our friend, man,' snapped Barty.

'Sorry, of course he was, but he wasn't really one of us, was he? His father was a bloody postman, for God's sake.'

'Sometimes, John, you take things too far.'

Sir John was about to answer when the phone interrupted him.

'Yes, who is it?'

'It's Callum, from the fish merchants. There's been some trouble,' he said, something in his voice suggesting he was holding back.

'Well, spit it out, man, what kind of trouble?' said Sir John, his annoyance clear in his voice.

'Three armed guys stormed in this morning, shot the place up before planting a bomb in the sorting room. Everything has gone, the place is in ruins.'

'What? It can't be. Couldn't you and Peeler stop them?' Sir John replied, his head spinning at the news.

'Sorry, boss, they were fast, I don't know, trained like a military unit. They shot Sidney in the shoulder with a bloody crossbow. It all happened so quickly. Hello, boss, you there?' said Callum Roper, puzzled when he got no reply.

Sir John's face fell as he lowered the phone to his lap.

'John, are you alright, old man? You've gone rather pale,' said Barty, sitting forward at the sight of him.

'It's them, Pearson and the others. They've just blown the fish merchants up. It's all gone.'

The news caused Barty to drop his cup in shock, two things putting fear into his heart.

Is Pearson coming for me? Oh my God, how are we going to pay Lars his money?

Regaining a little composure, Sir John lifted the phone back to his ear.

'What about the police, what did they say?'

'Don't worry, boss, we told them we smelled gas and

got everyone out before the place went up. They seemed to buy that.'

'And Mr Peeler's injury?'

'That's ok, I know a guy, he's a vet, but he patched him up good, he'll be ok.'

'Good man, thank you, Callum. I'll call you as soon as I figure out what to do,' said Sir John hanging up.

'How the hell did they know about the fish merchants? They're going to get us, John, I know it,' said Barty, his nerves frayed.

'Pull yourself together, Barty, the fish van was there the night the trouble started, they must have seen it. They're not going to come for us. If they were, they would have come straight here. They don't even know who we are, dear boy. Now calm down and let's figure out what we're going to do about Lars Silverman.'

'We pay him, we have to pay him,' said Barty, looking worse by the minute.

'Unless you have a million pounds sitting in your pocket, we don't have the money to pay him, do we? The cash is burnt to a cinder, we can't sell the drugs to pay him because a bunch of lunatic ex-SAS soldiers blew it up, and we've had to pay back most of the Sport of Kings hunt money to the clients who managed not to bloody die. No, we'll make a deal, buy us some time. We still have the Newton brothers' money and Nakatomi's and poor Dickies' in the pot. What's that, £200,000? We'll offer that to Lars and double the next deal to make the money back. Christ, I'll cut and bag the stuff here if I have to. Yes, that's what we'll do. Lars is a businessman, this is just a business blip, I'll call him now,' said Sir John, sitting upright as he convinced himself he could talk the common little Dutchman round.

Even Barty seem to perk up at the prospect of straightening the mess out.

Full of fresh bravado, Sir John scrolled through the contacts and called Lars Silverman.

'Sir John, so nice of you to call. I assume you have my money?' the Dutchman said in smooth-accented English.

'Indeed we do, Mr Silverman. We've had some production and supply issues which is causing a delay in converting the money into cash, but we will have it ready shortly. In the meantime, I'd like to double the next order, we'll even pay an extra 5% on the base rate for your inconvenience,' said Sir John, feeling in command again.

'That is a generous offer, Mr Riddlesworth, a surprise I must say. So you have no problems I should be concerned about?' Lars said. There was something cold and chilling in his voice.

'*Sir* John Riddlesworth, if you don't mind, old boy, mustn't forget one's standing,' Sir John said indignantly.

'Sorry, where are my manners, *Sir* John? I will come back to you on this matter shortly.'

The phone went dead before Sir John could answer. He placed it on the table beside him and smiled at Barty. 'You see, Barty old man, you just have to show these bloody foreigners who's boss.'

'Bravo, John, absolutely marvellous. I think I'm up for a round of golf after all,' Barty said, the colour coming back to his face.

Lars slid the phone back into his Armani suit pocket. 'What do you make of this, Jasper?' he said looking up at the six-foot-six solid Dutchman.

Jasper squatted down on his haunches, his blue suit

straining over his muscles as he picked up a couple of nails off the road behind the police tape.

'It is not gas, I think it is explosives, homemade, nail bomb,' he said straightening back up to tower over Lars as he pushed his floppy blonde hair out of his piercing blue eyes.

Another blond-haired suited man walked up beside them and handed Lars a newspaper. 'Here you are, boss.'

'Thank you, Bram,' Lars said, flicking it open to read the front page.

Pregnant woman escapes Norfolk Chief of Police's secret sadistic operating theatre.

Lars scanned the page, picking out more headlines.

His body found in hidden burnt-out basement on Harrington Farm, owned by Lord Bartholomew Harrington-Smythe.

Chief of Police Peter Metcalf's car found on the estate, with two kilos of cocaine in the boot and a large quantity of cash.

Lars turned and headed away from the burnt-out fish merchants towards the cars. Bram and Jasper followed without saying a word. The driver of the front vehicle got out and walked round to open the rear door for Lars and Jasper, while Bram got into the car behind with three other men.

'Claymoor Manor, Ruben.'

'Yes, boss,' said Ruben, driving slowly away from the burnt-out Riddlesworth Fish Merchants.

CHAPTER 45

After dropping Fergus and Smudge home, Danny finally pulled up outside his house. He yawned as he checked his appearance in the rear-view mirror. The last few days of tense activity and lack of sleep made him look ten years older. Remaining bits of crap in his unruly mop of dark hair and dirt round his neck and ears after his improvised wash in the services toilets wasn't helping his appearance. As tired as he was, he'd still taken the time to clean, strip and unload the guns, dropping the pieces in several places along the canal on his way home. Tucking the money wedge into his holdall, Danny pulled himself out of the car, making a mental note to get it valeted as soon as he'd had some sleep. He turned the key in the door and walked in, dumping his bag on the floor in the hall.

'Danny?' came Alice's voice from the kitchen.

'Hiya, gorgeous,' he said, noting her worried look as she hurried over to him. 'What's up?'

She threw her hands round him and hugged him tight.

He hugged her back, feeling her tremble beneath his hold. She pulled away, a tear falling from her eye.

'What's the matter?' said Danny softly.

'You didn't call last night and there's been all this stuff on the news about drug dealers and this poor woman who was tortured by this police chief, and I didn't know where you were,' she said, hugging him again.

'Hey, hey, I haven't seen any news. Me and Ferg found Smudge and got a little drunk last night, that's all,' Danny said with a reassuring smile that turned into an uncontrollable yawn.

'Yeah,' Alice said, taking a step back as she took in Danny's appearance. 'So why are you covered in mud and dressed in that shit outfit?'

Danny couldn't help smiling as he looked at her with her long, flaming red hair and burning green eyes. 'Ok, but it's over. Nothing to worry about, job's done, we got Smudge back and we're all ok.'

'It better be, Danny, I can't go through all that again,' she said, still looking worried.

Danny couldn't blame her; they'd met when he was working undercover for government man Howard and MI6. A corrupt general had sent a team to kill them over information her brother had. It didn't end well for the team.

'Don't worry, it's ok, I even got you a present,' he said, reaching for the bag and pulling the bundle of money out. 'Here you go. Go and buy some shoes or something,' he said breaking into a grin.

Her face softened and she moved in, standing on tiptoe as she kissed him gently.

'Christ, go and get a shower, you stink.'

'Yes ma'am. You can join me if you want,' he said as he kicked off his trainers and started padding up the stairs.

She looked at him and then at the money. Placing it on the table in the hall, she reached up and took his hand as he led her up the stairs.

CHAPTER 46

Barty and Sir John return to Claymoor Manor in a considerably better mood than they'd left. Over the course of eighteen holes, Sir John had worked out the details of their return to form and convinced both himself and Barty that in a few months' time they'd be back on top again. They could see Slade's Mercedes and a van by the house as they drove up the long drive. Sir John's butler, Michaels, opened the front door to greet them as they approached.

'I trust you had a good game, Sir. Mr Slade and his associates are waiting for you in the drawing room.'

'Very good, thank you, Michaels. Myself and Lord Smyth have business to discuss with Mr Slade and do not wish to be disturbed,' said Sir John, brushing past Michaels on his way through.

'As you wish, Sir.'

Barty and Sir John entered the large, panelled drawing room through high oak doors leading off from the grand hall. At the rear of the drawing room lay another set of doors adjoined to the kitchens and back staircase that would have originally been used by the servants of the house. Slade, Bill and Allen sat on French-style, hard-backed sofas set around a large, marble-topped coffee table.

'Vincent, gentlemen, I trust everything is taken care of at the farm?'

'It's all taken care of. Harper took the vehicles; they'll be crushed into little squares by now. As for the bodies, well, put it this way, the pigs won't have to eat for a week,' said Slade, talking as if it was a normal day's work.

'Did the police come and see you?' said Barty, his uncertainty returning.

'Yes, they turned up at the farmhouse. I showed them the rental agreement for the house and the fake marine biologist study papers. I told them we had nothing to do with the farm. They had a poke around the barn and the RIB then left.'

'Excellent. You see, Barty, everything is fine. Now onto business. We've all lost money here. I plan to double-up the next drop, we'll cut the product as fine as we can get away with and recoup our losses. Most of the deal will go to paying Lars Silverman back the lost money, but there will still be enough left for everyone. I have a couple of vacant lockups we can use to replace Riddlesworth Fish Merchants,' said Sir John, enjoying his own cleverness.

The smug look on his face fell like a lead balloon at the sound of a voice behind him.

'Bravo, Mr—sorry—*Sir* Riddlesworth, you've really got it all worked out,' came Lars's cold, slightly accented voice.

He'd entered silently as the men were talking and now walked coolly around them like a circling shark while the mountainous Jasper stood with Bram by the door. As the room went quiet, the doors at the far end of the drawing room opened. Ruben and Karl stepped in and shut the door behind them, standing side by side in a mirror to Jasper and Bram.

The tension grew. The only sound in the room was the *tap tap* of Lars's handmade Italian shoes on centuries-old oak.

'Lars, this is an unexpected surprise. Can I get you a drink, a brandy or scotch?' Sir John said, fighting back the panic he felt inside.

'No, thank you, I don't drink. I find it tends to cloud one's judgement, and I like my judgement to be crystal clear,' Lars said toying with the ornate rope that held the curtain back from the window, his demeanour calm and cool but his underlying menace never failing to come through.

'Well eh, what can I do for you?' Sir John said looking at Barty as Lars walked around the back of the chair he was in.

'Where is my money, Mr Riddlesworth?'

Sir John resisted the urge to correct Lars again regarding his title. 'Now listen here, old boy, I've told you the money is coming, let's arrange the next deal and—'

Standing behind Sir John, Lars flicked the rope curtain tie around Sir John's neck, pulling it and Sir John tight to the back of the chair. Across the marble-topped coffee table in the chair opposite, Allen reached inside his jacket for his gun. There were two loud pops from Ruben's gun, and Allen's body jerked like he'd been punched in the back. He sat upright with a surprised look on his face, his mouth opening to speak but only a trickle of blood dribbled out before he slumped back into the chair. Back across the coffee table, Sir John's face was turning purple and his eyes bulged in their sockets.

'Do you take me for a fool, Mr Riddlesworth, huh?' Lars said, leaning in close to his ear.

Sir John shook his head frantically as he tried to croak out a no.

'I know about the trouble in Norfolk and the explosion at the fish merchants. I also know you don't have my money,' Lars said letting go of the rope just as Sir John's eyes started rolling back into his head.

'Next question, who blew up my drugs?' continued Lars, directing his question to a horrified Barty as he continued to walk around the room calm and composed.

'It was Smith's friends. Metcalf said their names were Daniel Pearson and Fergus McKinsey. They stole your money from the dive site and burned it. We tried to get them, but they killed several of our men and got away. They blew up the fish merchants this morning in retaliation,' said Barty, blurting it out in fear.

'Thank you, Lord Bartholomew, that wasn't so hard was it?' Lars said, his eyes making contact with Slade's. Holding his gaze for a few seconds, he noted how calm and relaxed Slade looked sitting back in the chair.

'I have a certain reputation to uphold, and word of this embarrassment will spread like a cancer. If I do not seek retribution, my enemies will take it as weakness,' he said to Barty and Sir John.

'Yes, quite, by all means seek away, find the blasted fellows and kill them,' Sir John wheezed and coughed, his face slowly returning to its normal colour.

'You,' Lars said, whipping his head round to look at Slade. 'Do you know what these men look like?'

Slade sat forward, giving Lars a single nod as an answer.

'And you can find them?'

Slade pondered the question for a couple of seconds before answering, 'I'll find them for you, but I want to be the one who kills Pearson,' he said with an unreadable poker face.

'Excellent, then we don't need any of you gentlemen, do we?' Lars said, his ice cold blue eyes looking at Sir John.

The importance of his words didn't sink in for a few seconds as Sir John and Barty looked at each other. Bill got it straight away, reaching for his gun as fast as he could. A shot from Karl at the back of the room entered the back of Bill's head with a neat little hole before exiting out the front, taking most of his face with it. Flecks of blood and bits of brain sprayed across Barty and Sir John as they sat frozen in horror. Jasper walked slowly forward and double-tapped two bullets into Barty before turning and tapping two more into Sir John as he sobbed.

Lars looked back to Slade, interested to see him rise from his chair without the slightest reaction to the bloodshed.

'It would seem you are no stranger to death, Mr …?'

'Slade, Vincent Slade.'

'Slade, good. Let's go,' said Lars, walking around the bodies so as not to get blood on his expensive shoes.

As they exited the room into the hall, Michaels appeared from the rear of the house.

'Good evening, gentlemen. Is your meeting over?' he said, smiling.

'Yes, thank you,' said Lars as Jasper stepped past him and raised his gun towards Michaels' head.

CHAPTER 47

Parking in his reserved space, Danny walked to the front of the three-storey Victorian building. Ignoring the lift, he bounded up the stairs and pushed through the squeaky oak doors of Greenwood Security.

'Morning, Lucy,' he said, flashing her a wide smile which he knew always made her fluster.

'Oh, eh, yes, morning, Mr Pearson,' she replied, not knowing which way to look.

'It's Danny, how many times do I have to tell you, call me Danny,' he shouted cheerfully over his shoulder as he made his way to his office.

Pushing the door with *Danny Pearson, Director of Operations* on it, he hooked his jacket on the coat stand, and with a thump down into his office chair, he fired up his PC and started checking his emails.

'Morning, Daniel, glad to have you back. I take it you've sorted whatever you had to take a few days off for,' said the company's owner, Paul Greenwood, as he entered Danny's office.

'Morning, boss. Yeah, it was nothing really, ended up more of a reunion with my old unit,' said Danny, dismissing it casually.

'Really? That's nice. Did you hear about that terrible business in Norfolk while you were away?' Paul said, closing the office door and sitting himself down in the chair opposite Danny.

Danny sat twiddling a pen in his fingers as he pondered his response. He'd known Paul a lot of years, from way back when Paul had been one of the top intelligence officers. Supplying targets and mission info to Danny's SAS unit, the man was a walking think tank and had an almost supernatural ability to join the dots between events.

'Some situations can only ever go one way,' Danny replied, his dark eyes locked onto Paul's.

'You know, that's exactly what I told Howard at the club last night. He spent all of yesterday in meetings with the Prime Minister and the Director of the National Crime Agency. Apparently, they'd been investigating the influx of drugs being brought in along the Norfolk coast. They even had a guy undercover for six months as a tractor driver, watching people come and go on the RIBs and boats as he ferried them on and off Sea Palling beach,' said Paul with a knowing smile.

'Did they really? A tractor driver, well fancy that,' said Danny, returning the smile as he thought of the cantankerous old git he'd paid for information.

'Oh, and Howard said, 'Debt repaid.' He also said next time you go to save his life, let them shoot him. It would be less trouble all round,' Paul said, getting up to leave the room.

Danny thought of how he'd saved the high-ranking government man's life when a corrupt general had tried to kill them. Now they were even, and his get out of jail free card was all used up.

'Oh, and the young lady, Susan Wimple, the one in hospital after being horribly tortured? She wanted to thank the four Australian men who rescued her from that sadistic bastard Metcalf,' Paul said with a smile and a raised eyebrow before walking off towards his own office muttering, 'Australians, yeah right.'

'How is she? Did they managed to attach her hand?' Danny shouted after him.

'Yes, they don't know how much movement she'll get out of it though, too early to tell,' Paul shouted back.

The news brought a smile to Danny's face. Snapping out of it, he locked the last few days in the part of his brain that kept all the other horrors he'd seen from leaking out, and went back to checking through his emails.

The rest of the day passed uneventfully. He had a picture message from Chaz up in Scotland. He'd discovered the bundle of money Danny had put in the back of his van and was holding a wedge of notes in one hand and a thumbs up on the other one.

You can get the beers in when you get back. Danny sent back.

Roger that. came the message in return.

Feeling in a great mood, Danny gave Alice a call.

'Hello you,' she answered.

'Hi, honey, how do you fancy eating out tonight? Your choice where.'

'We could go up The Drum on Lea Bridge Road,' she said cheerfully.

'That's my girl, you can't beat a Wetherspoons,' Danny said, glad she hadn't picked some posh dressed-up restaurant.

'You better go down the gym tomorrow, you can work your dad bod off,' Alice said, teasing him.

'You what? Dad bod, what do you mean dad bod? I'm in the peak of physical fitness,' said Danny looking down at his stomach.

'Course you are, dear. I'll see you at six?'

'Yeah ok, bye love.'

Dad bod, me? No way.

CHAPTER 48

The next couple of days went by uneventfully. Danny got back into the humdrum of working life, scheduling security teams for various events in various countries. Alice's joking aside, he had put a few pounds on and had his kit bag with him for a workout at Pullman's Gym on the way home. Danny finished his meeting with Paul and shouted, 'See you tomorrow,' over his shoulder on the way out. He ran down the stairs enthusiastically, already looking forward to putting muscle against steel and raising the pulse and a sweat.

He left the building and walked to his car parked in its reserved spot. Popping the lock with the button on the key he pulled the door open a crack. A chill down his spine made him stop. The hairs on the back of his neck stood up and he could swear he could feel eyes boring into the back of his head. Turning round calmly, his dark eyes scanned people and cars along the road. Nothing out of the ordinary, no awkward strangers turning away, pretending not to look. For a full minute Danny stood stock still, his eyes picking out and analysing pedestrians and drivers as they passed. Still nothing unusual, nothing standing out.

He got in his car, still on edge. His heightened senses had served him well over the years, saving his life many times. Forced to let it go, Danny fired up the car and headed towards Walthamstow and Pullman's Gym.

As his powerful car drove off down the road with a throaty rumble, Slade rolled out of the coffee shop opposite and stood watching it for as long as it was visible.

Forty minutes later, with the feeling forgotten, Danny pulled up outside the gym, got out and pushed through the squeaky gym doors.

'Danny,' Dave said casually without looking up from the reception desk.

'Dave,' Danny replied, enjoying the ritual greeting.

'It's been a few weeks,' Dave said, slowly lifting his head to look Danny square in the eyes.

'Yes, it has.'

'You better fuck off and do some training then. You look soft as shit,' said Dave, dismissing him with a wave of his hand.

Danny chuckled. 'Yes sir.'

Just as he headed for the changing room, Dave called after him.

'Did your mate get hold of you?' he said, only mildly curious.

'My mate?' Danny said, turning back.

'Big bloke, six-foot, dark crew cut, dark eyes. Ex-forces type. He said you were an old mate from way back. Said he'd lost touch but remembered the gym you used and was trying to get back in touch with you.'

'And what did you say?' Danny said to Dave, his face turning into a frown.

'What am I, your secretary? I said you come in here sometimes, but I couldn't give him your address. He could have been anyone,' Dave said, looking across to check a customer's membership renewal details on the computer.

'Did you leave reception while he was here?' Danny said, staring at the names and addresses on the screen.

'What? What's with the twenty questions?' Dave replied, getting annoyed.

'Did you leave the fucking desk?' Danny's face was as hard as granite; his dark eyes looked at Dave in a way that he didn't want to challenge.

'Eh, yeah, some bloody kids were banging on the fire escape door out back. They'd run off by the time I opened it to have a look.'

With his mind racing, Danny turned and headed out the gym doors, his phone already to his ear.

'Hello handsome. Hang on a sec, there's someone at the door,' Alice said answering the phone.

'Alice, wait, stop. Don't answer that door, you hear me?' Danny shouted in desperation.

'What, why? What's wrong, Danny? You're scaring me,' she said, her voice trembling a little as she glanced out of the kitchen at the front door. A large, blurred, shadowy outline of a man filled the mosaic stained glass panels in its centre.

'It's ok, don't panic. Just listen to me, ok? Go out the back door, do it now,' Danny said, trying to sound calm while his heart was pounding in his chest.

'Ok,' Alice said, backing into the kitchen as the shadow at the front door knocked again.

'Go to the back of the garden and push the small fence panel behind the shed. Go, hurry.'

Alice did as Danny said. To her surprise, the panel was hinged and swung open like a small gate.

'Ok, I'm through,' she said, shutting it behind her.

'Good. Go down the side of the house — don't worry, the Robinsons should still be at work. You'll come out on Stainforth Road. The park's just around the corner; it'll be busy this time of day, you'll be safe there. I'll be five minutes.'

Before Alice could answer him, she heard the engine roar and the scream of tyres struggling for grip before the phone cut off. She came out on Stainforth Road and looked both ways, terrified of a repeat of when she'd first met Danny, and General Rufus McManus wanted them both dead. When no armed hit squads or menacing looking thugs presented themselves, she walked nervously to the park. Taking a seat on a bench near the children's play area, Alice felt safer surrounded by mums sitting watching their kids play. A tall blond-haired man wandered through the park, immaculately dressed in a designer suit, probably on his way home from his high-flying job in the city. He stopped and smiled and took a seat on the far end of her bench. Alice didn't pay him much attention; she was busy searching the road, waiting for Danny's appearance.

'Your boyfriend has caused us much inconvenience, Miss Campbell,' came Lars's slightly accented voice, cold and devoid of emotion.

She swung her head around to see him smiling at her, his ice-blue eyes staring unblinkingly at hers. She looked from side to side trying to decide whether to run or scream.

'What do you want?' she said, finding some inner strength.

'I would like you to give Mr Pearson a message. We are going to kill him and his little band of friends,' Lars said, still smiling.

The sound of Danny's sports car screaming its approach caused Alice to turn away, relief written across her face as Danny screeched to a halt and got out of the car in one fluid motion.

'Tell him yourse—' she said, turning back to find Lars had gone. She looked around the park, but he was nowhere to be seen.

'Yeah, just get everyone out, Ferg, this isn't over. Yep, I've called Smudge and Chaz. Look, I've got to go, I'll call you later,' Danny said putting down the phone as he hurried over to Alice.

She got up and ran over to him, hugging him tight as she finally let the tears flow.

'It's ok, I'm here,' said Danny, his eyes darting around the park from person to person, looking for someone out of place. No one presented themselves.

CHAPTER 49

After Alice told Danny about the terrifying conversation with the immaculately dressed Dutchman, the drive to Stratford was quiet and tense. Alice went from scared and upset to annoyed and resentful.

'You said this wouldn't happen again. Dodging killers and looking over my shoulder, scared at every noise or stranger walking down the street,' she finally said, her cheeks reddening as her emerald green eyes burned angrily.

'I'll deal with it,' was all Danny said, his mind busy running through his best course of action.

'I don't want you to deal with it. Normal boyfriends don't have to deal with people trying to kill them.'

'What do you want me to say, huh? It's happened, I'll deal with it. Ok?' Danny growled back, instantly regretting snapping back at her.

A heavy silence fell on the car again and lasted until he pulled up outside Alice's tiny terrace house in Stratford. With a tear in her eye, she got out.

'I love you, but I don't think I can live like this, always looking over my shoulder, worrying if you're going to make it home or if I'm going to get a phone call saying you're dead,' said Alice, shutting the car door and hurrying off inside before he could reply.

Danny watched her go. There was so much he wanted to say, but his thoughts were dominated by the problem at hand. Banging the steering wheel in frustration, Danny spun the car around and tore off down the street. He only had two names from Norfolk: Vincent Slade and Lord Bartholomew Harrington-Smythe. He needed to find out who the Dutchman was.

Perhaps Smudge knows.

'Smudge, where are you, bud?' said Danny on the car's hands-free.

'I'm at my sister's flat. Ferg's here too,' said Smudge.

'Good, I've just got to pick something up from the house then I'll be over.'

'Alright, brother, be careful.'

'Always am,' Danny replied, hanging up and checking his mirrors for tails.

After driving past his house twice, Danny came around the block for a final time and parked outside. Climbing out of the car, he stood for a moment scanning up and down the road for anything out of the ordinary. Nothing, all was quiet.

He got to the front door to find it open a crack. Danny folded himself to one side and swung across to look through the living room window. All clear. Squatting down so his body didn't present a visible target through the mosaic stained glass window panes, Danny put his ear to the crack in the door. Breathing shallowly, he tuned out the sounds of the suburbia around him and concentrated on the noises from the house.

Nothing.

No, wait. A *click*, a *chink*.

Somebody's in the kitchen.

With millimetre-at-a-time control, Danny pushed the door open enough to get a glimpse into the hall. It was clear, but he could still hear someone moving around in the kitchen. Moving in through the gap, Danny reached down and silently slid the baseball bat he kept in the umbrella stand out. Holding it up ready to hit a home run, he moved towards the kitchen, treading lightly, rolling his feet from heel to toe to make no noise.

There it was again, a *chink*. Rocking slightly, he breathed deeply as he prepared his leg muscles to explode into action.

Locate, strike, don't get shot. One, two, three.

The speed and power of Danny's movement was astounding. He was in the middle of the kitchen in a split-second, swinging the bat at his located target with enough force to take their head off. It was when he was inches away from contact that recognition kicked in and he pulled the bat short of striking, the gust from its movement blowing the man's hair out of place.

'Good evening, Daniel, good of you to join me. I thought you'd forgotten where you live with all that driving around in circles,' said the secretive government man with not so much as a blink at Danny's entrance.

'Howard, for fuck's sake, can't you just knock on the door like any normal person?' said Danny, dumping the bat on the table in front of Howard's cup of tea.

'And where would the fun be in that?' said Howard, picking his cup up to take a sip.

'Cup the crap, Howard, I'm kinda busy, what do you want?' Danny said, letting out a sigh as he plonked down in a chair opposite.

'Dear boy, your recent business is what brings me here,' said Howard, reaching down to his side to pick up a briefcase. He clicked it open on his lap and took out a folder before looking up at Danny. 'Be a good chap and move the toothpick.'

Danny picked up the baseball bat begrudgingly and stood it up against the wall.

'Thank you,' said Howard, opening the file on the table.

'Now, I'm not sure what or who you know, but the National Crime Agency has been taking a keen interest in our friends from Norfolk. Not something they have involved me in — my interests, as you know, are usually taken up with our more volatile international acquaintances. That is until a couple of days ago when these men ended up on the wrong end of a bullet.' Howard placed down several pictures of the men killed at Claymoor Manor.

'These two gentlemen are Sir John Riddlesworth and Lord Bartholomew Harrington-Smythe, the rest are the drug smugglers posing as marine biologists you met in Norfolk.'

'That one, the Lord, he was on Metcalf's phone when I got the girl out,' Danny said, taking a closer look at the photo. 'Why haven't I heard about any of this on the news?'

'Because Lord Bartholomew and Sir John both have friends in high places and Lord Bartholomew is related to the Queen. Imagine the questions that would be raised if the press found out what these two have been up to. Shit sticks, and certain men and women in parliament and royal circles do not wish to get covered in it,' said Howard, collecting the pictures back up.

'So who killed them? The Dutch guy who threatened Alice?'

'I rather think *you* did, inadvertently. The demolition job you did on their setup in Norfolk and the destruction of the cutting room in Chelsea cost them dearly and was a source of great embarrassment to this man,' Howard said, placing a photo of Lars Silverman on the table.

'The Dutchman?'

'Lars Silverman, the Dutchman, is suspected of supplying over half of the UK's cocaine. He has a reputation for murdering people who fail him and taking revenge on those who cross him. Charming man who's currently at the top of the NCA and the Dutch DEA's most wanted list,' Howard said, placing more pictures beside Lars'.

'Why don't they arrest him then?'

'Nobody's lived long enough to testify against him. Right, this gentleman you know. Vincent Slade, ex-Navy, Special Boat Service, location unknown, but we think he may be with Lars. This rather large gentleman is Jasper Van Beek, Lars's right-hand man. We don't know who this gentleman is,' Howard said, tapping a picture of Bram. 'I didn't get a chance to ask him; he's in the cupboard under your stairs with his neck broken.'

'Did you kill him?' Danny asked Howard, surprised.

'Certainly not, I have people like you for that. My man caught him snooping around the place and killed him when he pulled a gun,' said Howard, brushing a bit of lint off his tailor-made suit trousers.

'Ok, this is all very nice, but why are you telling me this?' said Danny, eyeing Howard with suspicion.

'The powers that be want the whole thing to go away and they want Lars Silverman out of the picture. Officially their hands are tied. Unofficially they want Lars dead along with all his associates. As you made a splendid start in Norfolk and Lars actively wants you dead, I thought you would be the ideal man to assist me in this matter,' said Howard, tidying the photos back into the file.

Danny sat back, thinking it through for a minute.

'I need weapons and payment,' he finally said, his face hardening and dark eyes fixing on Howard's.

'Of course. Tell me what you need and I'll get it to you. As for the money, name your price and I'll see what I can do,' Howard said, standing to leave.

'One thing.'

'Yes,' said Howard at the kitchen door.

'How did you know I was on my way back here?' Danny said, puzzled.

'I knew you'd come back to get that Glock 17 you've got hidden under the floorboards in your bedroom,' Howard said with a smug smile. He turned and made for the front door without waiting for Danny's reply. 'Don't worry about the man in the cupboard; a cleanup crew's on the way, he'll be gone in a jiffy. You might find his gun and the phone in his pocket useful though,' Howard shouted back over his shoulder before shutting the front door.

CHAPTER 50

Danny got to Wandsworth just as the sun dipped below the tower blocks, leaving the entrance doors shrouded in orange-lit shadows. The council tower block that Smudge's sister Kelly lived in had seen better days, and last time he and Chaz were there they'd had to teach a local gang a lesson just to get in. Thankfully the estate was quiet as he approached the intercom by the door.

'Hello?' came Kelly's scratchy voice through the metal panel.

'Hi, Kelly, it's Danny, are Fergus and Smudge there?'

'Yes, unfortunately, come on up,' she said as the door lock buzzed open.

Avoiding the lift, Danny ran up six flights of stairs and wandered along the corridor to Kelly's door. It opened before he had a chance to knock on it, Smudge's grinning face standing in its place.

'You took your bloody time,' he said walking back into the flat so Danny could follow.

'Yeah, I had a visitor,' said Danny, entering the small lounge.

'Hello Danny,' said Kelly with a smile.

'Alright Kel, Fergus?' Danny said, taking a seat.

'Don't keep us in suspense, what's happened? It better be good. The missus is going nuts after I threw her and the kids in the car and drove them to her mum's,' said Fergus.

'Ok, I'll tell you what I know,' said Danny, leaning forward in the chair.

He told them about the guy at the gym who he suspected was Slade, and how Lars had threatened Alice in the park. Then he ran through his conversation with Howard at his house, finishing with Bram's body in his cupboard under the stairs as he pulled out a Glock 17 and Bram's Smith & Western handgun and phone and placed them on the coffee table.

'So, what do you say?' Danny said, as Smudge and Fergus looked at him blankly.

'Er, exactly how much money are we talking about here?' said Smudge, finally breaking into a smile.

'I was going for £100k each. If they want this guy as badly as Howard says, they'll pay it.'

'Fuck me, I'm in,' said Smudge with a grin.

'Ferg?' Danny said, turning to him.

'What's the alternative, stay in hiding until you bastards get him or he gets you? I'm in,' Fergus said, getting up and shaking his empty beer can at them.

'Yes please, mate,' said Danny.

'Get one for me,' shouted Smudge from the sofa.

'Make yourselves at home, why don't you,' said Kelly from the kitchen.

'Sorry sis, we'll be out of your hair soon,' said Smudge, pulling a face to the other two.

'What about Chaz?' said Fergus, passing the beer cans around.

'He's on his way back from Scotland. I tried to tell him he'd be safer off up there, but you know Chaz, he wasn't having any of it. He'll be here in a few hours,' said Danny, his conversation stopping abruptly when Bram's phone rang. They all looked at the coffee table, at the withheld caller ID, then back up at each other. Danny grabbed it and pressed the answer button, holding it to his ear without saying a word.

'Bram, it's Jasper. Where are you? The boss is in a real bad mood and wants you back here now,' said Jasper, his deep voice emphasising more of an order than a question.

Remembering what Lars had said to Alice, Danny answered. 'You and your boss have caused us a lot of inconvenience, Jasper. I would like you to give Mr Silverman a message. We are going to kill him and all of his friends, including you.'

Danny hung up without waiting for a reply.

'That should put the cat amongst the pigeons.'

'Why did you tell him we're coming for him?' Smudge said, puzzled.

'Angry men make mistakes, Smudge, and I've got a feeling Lars will be doing his nut about now. Right, let's make a plan of attack and a shopping list for Howard.'

CHAPTER 51

'Well, where is he?' shouted Lars from the other side of the warehouse.

'He's gone, boss, Pearson got him,' said Jasper, lowering the phone slowly from his ear.

'What, how? What did he say?' growled Lars marching over to Jasper, his ice-blue eyes burning angrily.

'The bastard said he's going to kill us all,' said Jasper, waiting for his boss's inevitable explosion.

'How dare he? Who the fuck does he think he is, threatening me? Fucker,' Lars shouted pulling his gun out of its shoulder holster and shooting the tracksuited drug runner standing beside him five times in the chest before anyone could figure out what was going on.

The rest of the youths looked on horrified, too scared to move. Lowering the gun, Lars walked up and down in front of them, his calm persona returning.

'My apologies, that was uncalled for,' he said sliding the gun back into its holster. 'I want this man found. DO YOU HEAR ME? You are my eyes and ears on the street. You go out and find Daniel Pearson and his friends and find them quickly. He has disrupted my business which has cost me money. When it costs me money, it costs you money. Now go!' Lars said, waving them off. They didn't need much prompting and vanished out of the building as fast as they could. Once they'd gone, Lars turned his attention to a muscular-looking black guy with dreadlocks standing in front of his sidekicks.

'You!' Lars yelled, staring at him. 'What's his name, Jasper?' said Lars quietly to the man mountain beside him.

'Winston, boss.'

'You, Winston, you keep your boys on their toes, right? I want these men found quickly, ok? Here, this is for your trouble, and take that with you when you leave,' Lars said, pointing at the dead body before pulling a big wedge of notes out of his jacket pocket and handing it to Winston.

'Ya man, no worries. If they're in London, we'll find them,' Winston said, breaking into a wide grin that showed off his four gold front teeth.

Lars nodded and walked to the cars. He got in the back of the one in front, while Jasper got in the front passenger seat next to Slade.

'Drive to the house. Jasper, you show him the way,' said Lars, already on the phone to his business associates. 'Nikki, it's good to talk to you. No, the London thing is a temporary setback. I'm here now, straightening it all out. Two, three weeks at the most and London will be back at full capacity.'

'Head to Knightsbridge,' Jasper said gruffly to Slade.

Turning the car around the dead runner and Winston's men, Slade weaved between the warehouse pillars and headed out the roller door. Ruben and three other guys followed closely in the other car.

Winston watched them go before turning to his crew.

'Fucking crazy Dutchman, wouldn't want to get on the

wrong side of that motherfucker,' said Winston, laughing as he waved the wedge of cash in the air.

'Ain't that right, Trevor?' said one of his sidekicks to the dead body on the ground.

The comment caused the crew to fall about laughing.

'Go get your car, man. We'll weigh him down and dump him in the Thames later tonight,' said Winston to his man.

A couple of minutes later a bright orange Fiat Panda drove in through the roller door and circled to a halt beside them.

'What the fuck is that?' said Winston as all eyes fell on Ade.

'It's a Panda innit,' replied Ade.

'I can fucking see that, Adrian. What the fuck are you doing driving it?'

'Me BM's in the garage, they gave me this as a loaner while it's being fixed,' said Ade with a blank expression on his face.

'Fuck it, open the boot,' said Winston, shaking his head.

Ade did as Winston said and four of them picked up their dead runner, bending him in two to get him in the tiny boot. Dave tried several times to slam the boot shut, but the youth's arm kept falling out and getting trapped in it. They all looked at each other, then raised their trainered feet, stamping on the body until they could shut the boot down. Still laughing at Ade, they all squeezed into the tiny two-door car and drove it out of the warehouse.

'Fuck's sake, Ade, this is fucking embarrassing,' grumbled Winston.

CHAPTER 52

They passed the Rolex watch dealers, then the Lamborghini dealers, then the Maserati dealers, and then Harrods before Jasper spoke.

'Next left,' he said to Slade without looking over.

Slade turned into Beaufort Gardens with its six-storey Georgian townhouses lining either side of a wide road. Parking bays ran down the centre in between a row of mature trees.

'This one, number twenty-three. Pull up here,' said Jasper, tilting his head to check the second car in the wing mirror was behind them.

Jasper was out first, flexing out his six-foot six-inch frame as his cold ice-blue eyes checked the surrounding area. Satisfied, he moved to the back door and opened it for Lars who moved straight past him and up the steps between two pillars that supported the porch and balcony above. He entered, leaving the door open for his entourage to follow. When everyone was inside the marble-floored hall with its grand staircase spiralling the way up to the sixth floor, Lars spoke.

'There are guest rooms on the fifth and sixth floors for you. Jasper, I want one of them on this door at all times,' said Lars, wandering through to the lounge.

'Yes, boss,' said Jasper, following him.

'Send Ruben out for food, steak, not the cheap shit,' Lars said, sitting on a leather Chesterfield sofa. He pulled the guns from their shoulder holsters and placed them on the coffee table. Picking up the remote, he turned a massive TV on.

'How long do you think we're going to be here?' said Jasper.

'Not long, Jasper, a week at most. After we kill Pearson, we finish setting up distribution and go home.'

'Good, I hate this fucking country with its titles and arrogance and stiff upper lip,' said Jasper moving to the drinks cabinet and pouring himself a whiskey. He shook the decanter towards Lars, who nodded his head.

'Don't worry, my friend, we will be home before you know it,' replied Lars, taking the whiskey off him.

'*Proost*.'

'*Proost*,' said Lars, raising his glass to return the toast.

Slade tapped his way up the marble staircase, glancing in at the plush furnished rooms as he ascended. He couldn't imagine the cost of a place like this. A flat in this area of Knightsbridge would cost over a million. Moving to a bedroom at the back of the house on the sixth floor, he looked out the window at the houses and gardens of some of the most expensive real estate in the country.

Kill Pearson, get in with Lars Silverman, run London for him and get me some of this.

The thought put a flicker of a smile across his face, just for a second before his usual cold, unreadable expression returned.

CHAPTER 53

Rolling over on Kelly's sofa, Danny picked up his old G-Shock watch, blinking the sleep away until he could focus: 08:30. Sitting slowly upright, he scratched his wavy mop of dark hair and looked across at Chaz asleep in the chair opposite. It had been two in the morning by the time he'd driven all the way from Scotland, and then they'd had beers and talked about Lars, and then more beers. He got up and walked into the small kitchen, clicking on the kettle. As he looked around the cupboards for more coffee cups, his phone buzzed in his pocket. Taking it out, he selected the message from an unknown number.

Blue van in the car park, key's inside the fuel flap. Equipment's in the back. The money men thought you were asking more than your worth, I told them you were not. Do not prove me wrong. Good luck.

'Everything alright?' said a bleary-eyed Chaz as he entered the kitchen.

'Yes, mate, kit's outside. Coffee?' Danny said, shaking the jar at him.

'Great. Yeah, coffee, strong. I think it'll take a full English to clear this head.'

'Get this down your neck while I wake the others and we'll find a cafe,' Danny said, pouring a cup for each of them and one for Smudge's sister, Kelly.

Less than an hour later they were ready to leave. Danny had a whip round for Kelly for putting up with them. They all put a grand in from their Norfolk cash and Smudge put it in the little money tin she kept in the kitchen cupboard for bills for her to find later.

'I don't want to know what you're up to, just let me know you're all ok when it's finished,' she said as they left the flat.

'Cheers sis. When this is over I'll get you out of this shitty flat and into something nice, I promise,' Smudge said in an uncharacteristic display of emotion.

'Whatever, just don't get yourself killed, you dozy prick,' she shouted back with a smile.

They approached the blue van with care, the four of them watching in all directions just in case of prying eyes. If they got caught by the police with the contents of the bag in the back of the van, they could all go down for a ten-stretch. Danny fished the keys from the fuel flap and slid the side door open. They all huddled around and unzipped the bag, checking the contents before zipping it back up again.

'Looks good to me,' said Fergus getting into the front passenger seat. Chaz slid in next to him on the twin seat while Danny hopped in the driving seat.

'What? Come on, guys, not again,' said Smudge climbing in the back grudgingly.

'You snooze you lose, Smudge. Now get in the back and quit grumbling. First stop cafe, then we get to work.'

Pulling himself out of the swimming pool in the basement of his Beaufort Gardens house, Lars picked up the large fluffy white towel and dried himself off. He felt strong and alive after working out on the weights in his fully equipped gym next to the pool, followed by a steam sauna and a twenty-minute swim. He pushed a panel in the wall, popping it forward to reveal a private staircase leading to his bedroom on the second floor. Climbing the stairs, Lars passed the concealed door to the dining room. He continued up past a door to his private office on the first floor, and up to the second floor. Pushing a heavy wooden panel forward, he entered the master bedroom. Ten minutes later Lars descended the main staircase, immaculately dressed in a charcoal Armani suit. He entered the drawing room, picked up the morning papers and sat browsing the headlines.

'Jesus, look at these idiots,' said Jasper eyeing Winston, Ade and the other two misfits getting out of the Fiat Panda outside the house.

'Don't judge a book by its cover, my friend. They have the best network to sell our product, and more eyes on the street than anyone else to find Pearson and his friends,' said Lars wandering over to the window to see the out-of-place group approaching the multimillion-pound house in tracksuits, gold chains and baseball hats. 'Mmm, they do look like fucking idiots though. I'll grant you that.'

'Yo, Mr Silverman,' said Winston, flashing his gold teeth as he swaggered into the room ahead of his crew.

'Mr Hacker, have you any news for me?' said Lars, cutting him dead with a cold look.

'Eh, yeah man, we've got eyes everywhere, the minute

they surface I'll let you know, sweet,' said Winston, with animated arm gestures.

'I have a better idea,' said Lars, turning to Slade and Ruben standing in the doorway. 'Time to prove your worth, Mr Slade. Take Ruben, two others and a car, and go with Mr Hacker. The minute they locate Pearson and friends you may kill them.'

'Yes boss,' said Slade, a flicker of a smile flashing across his face.

'Get this done quickly, gentlemen, I'm not known for my patience,' said Lars, as the group of men turned and headed for the door.

'You think I should go with them?' said Jasper, shaking his head as he watched Winston's crew squeezing back into the Panda before heading out of the treelined cul-de-sac followed by Slade's men in a black BMW 4x4.

'No, Jasper, I have to organise what's needed to prepare the warehouse for the first delivery. We will use the Dutch-Grow factory to replace the lost dive site. They can pack the drugs inside the fertiliser bags; it'll throw the sniffer dogs off at the container ports.'

'Yes boss,' said Jasper, moving away from the window.

'Don't look so down, Jasper. When we finish at the warehouse I have a little insurance policy to pick up. Now go and get the men, we leave in five minutes,' Lars said, leaving the room without waiting for an answer.

CHAPTER 54

Danny drove his BMW M4 slowly across London. He had the window down and music playing loudly as he headed down Walthamstow High Street.

'You guys noticed anything?' he said into the throat mic hidden by his zipped-up jacket.

'Only your shocking taste in music,' came Chaz's response through his earpiece.

Danny stuck his middle finger up in the middle of the car and heard chuckles over his earpiece from the guys following in the blue van a little way back.

'Keep your eyes peeled, guys, I'm going to swing by the gym.'

'Roger that,' replied Chaz.

Turning off the high street, Danny pulled up outside Dave Pullman's gym. He ignored the blue van that drove past and parked up fifty metres down the road. Getting out, Danny walked casually to the entrance, taking in his surroundings as discreetly as possible.

'Two, corner of the high street,' he said as he entered the gym.

'I see them, I think they're just hanging about. Hold on, one's just eyeballed you. Yep, he's going for his phone.'

'Roger that,' said Danny, moving over to Big Dave on reception.

'You alright, son? You went off in a right hurry the other day,' said Dave, frowning.

'Yeah, I'm fine. That fella who came in looking for me, have you seen him since?'

'Nah, but there's been a couple of lowlifes hanging around outside since he was here,' said Dave, sensing there was some sort of trouble brewing.

'Thanks, Dave. I'll see you soon, mate,' said Danny with a smile as he left.

Heading out the door Danny got back in the car, started it and waited.

'Hold tight, they're still chattering,' came Fergus's voice.

'Roger that,' said Danny, watching the two youths in the mirror.

He didn't have to wait long before two more youths dressed head to toe in Adidas and Nike rolled up on a scooter. The one with his phone still glued to his ear pointed in Danny's direction, causing two helmeted heads to swing his way.

'Contact, I'm moving out,' said Danny, indicating then pulling out.

'Roger that.'

Danny drove past the van, casting an eye in the rear-view mirror now and then to make sure the scooter was following. Leaving a decent gap, the blue van pulled out and followed at the rear.

'I'd love to run the little shits over right now,' said Chaz, resisting the temptation.

'All in good time, mate. I'm going to take a slow drive up to the petrol station on Lea Bridge Road and fill up, give them time to get their act together. You guys go on and get the welcome ready,' said Danny, chugging along in second gear with the scooter buzzing along like an annoying mosquito behind him.

'Roger that,' said Chaz, peeling off left at the next crossroads.

After taking the long way round, Danny pulled into the garage. He got out and filled the car to the brim. Pretending to browse the shop before paying for the fuel, Danny kept an eye out the window. The scooter had parked up a little way along and the pillion passenger had been on his mobile ever since. Just as Danny went to pay, a Fiat Panda and a big black BMW 4x4 pulled up beside them. Windows went down and conversations took place. Danny couldn't see who was in the BMW because of the heavy tint on the windows, but the four guys sandwiched in the Panda looked like lowlife street criminals. He paid and left, not looking directly at the vehicles, just keeping them in his peripheral vision. The scooter left before Danny drove out, leaving the Panda doing a poor job of following inconspicuously, with the BMW doing a rather better job behind it.

Here we go, let's get this show on the road.

'ETA five minutes,'

'Roger that, come on in,' said Chaz, the sound of a door being forced in the background.

Danny took a five-minute detour with his shadows in tow, eventually turning into the car park of an old disused theatre.

The Panda and the BMW drove past and parked up

further down the road. Danny continued to keep up the pretence that he hadn't seen them and walked around the side of the building, entering via a forced fire door. Two minutes later, the Panda and BMW drove into the car park. Eight men got out and followed Slade to the boot of the BMW, each one taking it in turns to pick from the selection of MP5 automatic weapons and pump-action shotguns.

'Winston, take your guys and find a way in around the back. Me and Ruben will go in the side door, and you two take the front. Nobody kills Pearson but me,' said Slade, his face taut and eyes blazing.

They nodded in agreement and fanned out, heading to the different entrances.

CHAPTER 55

'Sound check,' said Danny looking down at the barely visible stage from the upper circle of seating.

'Arsehole.'

'Wanker.'

'Tosser.'

'Reading you dickheads loud and clear. Everyone in position?' Danny said, flipping a dust-covered red velvet seat down. He sat down in the darkness, leaned forward and rested his elbow on the balcony, steadying the MP5 assault rifle as he moved his head in unison with its red laser targeting dot, his vision through the latest high-tech night vision goggles in almost daylight clarity.

'In position. Targets approaching front entrance. Over,' said Chaz, calm and business-like.

'Covering rear exits. Over,' said Smudge.

'In place. Hostiles entering side door. Over,' said Fergus, his breathing slow and voice hushed.

'Roger that. Disable and disarm if possible. Anyone gets eyes on Lars, sound off.'

Winston scratched his head as he stood with his three mates looking at the locked rear doors.

'Go on, Joe, give it some welly, geez, kick it in,' he said to the largest member of his crew.

Joe swaggered his way to the front. 'Stand back, boys, let the man go to work.'

He bounced on his toes a couple of times then ran full pelt at the door, planting his foot halfway up it with a loud boom. The door didn't move an inch. Joe grimaced and limped back towards the others as they all fell about laughing.

'Shit, I think I've bust me fucking leg,' Joe said over dramatically.

'Move out the way, man, I'll show you how it's done,' said Winston, swinging a pump-action shotgun up. 'Yippee-ki-yay, motherfuckers!'

He pulled the trigger and blew a football-sized hole where the lock used to be. The door swung inwards as the crew cheered and whooped.

'Let's go waste a white dude,' said Ade, dodging left and right before swinging in through the door in a poor imitation of a tactical entrance. He found himself in the storage area behind the stage. Apart from the light from the blown-open door, the room was pitch black.

'Come on,' he shouted, turning to look back for the others.

'Psst, not a sound, understand?' said Smudge, jamming the barrel of his silenced Glock into the base of Ade's skull.

'Yeah, yeah,' said Winston, swaggering in with the other two behind him. 'Fucking dark in here, man. Ade, where are you, geez?' he said, clicking his phone light on and holding it up high in one hand as he swung his shotgun around nervously with the other. 'Ade?'

'Ade, stop fucking about, bro, where are you?' said Joe at the back, turning his phone light on.

As they passed the long-forgotten boxes and screen sets, Smudge rolled out from behind one, grabbing Joe firmly by the back of his jacket while pushing the silenced barrel against the side of his head.

'Ok, boys, keep it nice and calm. Place your weapons on the floor, slowly does it,' said Smudge, peeping out from behind the cover of Joe, barely visible to the others.

'Fuck, man. That ain't happening, blood, you drop your weapon,' snarled Winston, raising his shotgun as he tried to get a fix on Smudge past Joe.

'Winston, brother, what you doing, man? Put the gun down,' said Joe, his eyes going wide as he panicked.

'Put the gun down, son, I don't want to hurt you,' said Smudge, his voice calm and commanding.

'Who you calling son? I don't fucking know you. Ah, fuck dis,' growled Winston, losing his temper and pulling the trigger as Joe looked at him in disbelief.

The impact from the shotgun tore a large hole in Joe's chest, killing him instantly as it knocked him and Smudge backwards. As they fell, Smudge shot his head out sideways and locked his gun arm on Winston. He double-tapped two into Winston's chest and two more in the last member of the crew as he thudded to the ground with Joe's lifeless body flopped on top of him.

'Smudge, come in, Smudge. Are you ok?' came Danny's voice over the earpiece.

'Affirmative. Shots fired, three dead, one detained.'

'Roger that, Smudge. Join Chaz, we've got hostiles on the front doors. Over.'

'Roger that,' said Smudge, rolling Joe off him and getting up.

CHAPTER 56

The two men Slade sent to the front doors took a more cautious approach: not military but gangland savvy. The glass on the entrance doors had long since been covered with plywood sheeting, and the broken locks secured with a hasp and staple, a chunky padlock securing them through the ring. But the fixings were old and the plywood had rotted. It only took a couple of cracks from the butt of an assault rifle and the fixings gave way. The men opened the doors cautiously and entered, quickly moving to each side of the old ticket booth in the foyer. Waving each other on, they pushed through the left and right entrance doors to the theatre's stalls. Once inside, one man crouched in the aisle, looking across the twenty seats to his colleague doing the same on the other aisle. They stayed put for a while as their eyes got used to the darkness.

'Hostiles entering stalls,' said Chaz, tucked between the seating in the pitch black of the right side.

'Eyes on. I'll take the one on the right. Over,' said Smudge.

'Roger that.'

Danny was still up in the circle seating, so he couldn't see who Smudge and Chaz were talking about but he wasn't worried. One on one in the dark with those two, they didn't stand a chance.

He was concentrating on covering Fergus and the side door when it flew open unexpectedly. Sunlight from outside overloaded his night vision, blinding him for a second. In the meantime, Ruben poked his MP5 around the door frame and sprayed the inside with covering fire, causing Fergus to dive flat on his belly between the seats as bits of red velvet and foam puffed up into the air like confetti. Using the cover, Slade flew in and ducked off towards the stage. He crouched beside it and fired three bursts to keep heads down while Ruben ran across to join him.

Up in the circle seating, the stars cleared from Danny's eyes. He slid the rifle around and aimed the laser dot at Slade. As it ran across Slade's chest, Danny squeezed the trigger. At the same time, Slade sprang back with catlike reactions. The bullets missed, punching neat holes through the stage. In a flash Slade had his Heckler & Koch MP5 rifle up and firing, chipping splintered lumps off the balcony in front of Danny as he ducked. When the volley finished, Danny looked back over, his eyes locking with Slade's. Even in the semidarkness he could feel the intense hatred in his stare. Then he was gone, moving like lightning to the storage rooms behind the stage.

'Ferg, you alright?' Danny said.

'Yeah, fuck, I'm ok,' he replied huffing and puffing as he squeezed back up from between the seats.

Seeing Slade and Ruben's explosive entrance through the side door, the two men in the aisles gained confidence and started working their way down towards the stage. At the same time, Fergus popped up from between the seats with his back to them. Before Chaz could warn him, one of Slade's men shot Fergus in the back with a pump-action shotgun. The blast hit Fergus like a ton of bricks, sending him crashing over the seating in front like someone had pulled him on a bungee cord. Without a word being said, the two men shook and dropped to the sound of multiple metallic pings from Chaz and Smudge's silenced Glocks.

'Ferg's hit,' said Smudge, leaping over the seating to get to him.

'Ferg, talk to me, mate,' said Chaz, not far behind, with his gun up towards the stage in case of more gunfire from Slade and Ruben.

'I'm on my way down. Talk to me, guys,' said Danny, ripping off the night vision and running up the aisle to the exits.

'He's not moving. Ferg, come on, Fergus, don't you fucking die on me,' said Smudge, lifting him out from between the seats.

'How bad is it?' said Danny, bursting through the doors by the ticket booth.

'I don't know, it's too dark, I can't s—'

'Aargh, Jesus, what hit me?' said Fergus, dazed.

'Hold tight, mate, don't move,' said Chaz, holding up his phone and putting the light on.

He could see blood on Fergus's jacket sleeve and a hole in the back of the jacket. When he lifted it up, he was glad to see the back of a shot-peppered bulletproof vest.

'Good lad,' said Danny, coming up beside them.

'Where's the blood coming from?' said Smudge.

'I think my arm caught some of the shot, because it hurts like a son of a bitch,' said Fergus, still feeling winded.

'Take him outside and check his arm, Chaz. Me and Smudge'll get Slade and the other one.'

With his arm around Fergus's waist, Chaz helped him up the aisle and out into the foyer.

'Take the left, Smudge, and be careful,' Danny said, peeling off to the right of the stage.

'Standard sweep, Smudge. If it moves, shoot it.'

'Roger that.'

CHAPTER 57

'Take cover, Smudge, I'm going to light the place up,' said Danny, spotting a big grey fuse board and circuit breaker.

He pulled the big red handle down with a clunk. The round wall lights came on, lighting the backstage storage area dimly. Through the stage curtains, Danny could see the bright lights on the performing area and the house lights beyond turning the grey bleakness into a sea of red velvet seating. A rustle and mumbling behind some old theatre sets drew his attention. Poking his head around, Danny saw Ade laying on his side, his hands and feet zip tied behind him and a rag taped in his mouth. He stared at Danny with wide, scared eyes, breathing a sigh of relief when Danny moved off out of sight.

Where are you, Slade? Where would I be?

Moving silently, his eyes darting, searching for movement, Danny looked through the gap in the curtains at the stage. Some dust glistened as it fell from up high, sparkling like glitter as it crossed the beams of the bright stage lights. Danny looked up, but the brightness made the metal walkway and lighting rails beyond too dark to see.

'He's up in the lighting gallery, I'm going up,' whispered Danny as he moved to a metal spiral staircase at the side of the stage.

'Roger that,' said Smudge, tucking himself into the curtained area on the opposite side of the stage. He shielded his eyes with his hand, trying to get a fix on Slade. Still looking up, he heard a footstep no more than a foot away on the other side of the curtain. Turning to face it, Smudge floated the barrel of his gun millimetres from the fabric as he tried to get a fix on the person on the other side. The sound of the footsteps vanished, and Smudge was starting to think whoever it was had backed silently away. To his surprise, a hand pushed the material forward and grabbed the wrist of his gun hand. Smudge swung to one side instinctively as a blast of automatic fire punched a circle of bullet holes where his chest had just been. When the volley ceased, Smudge threw his free hand into the curtain, grabbing tightly when it hit the metallic shape of Ruben's assault rifle. Locked in each other's grip, Smudge drew his head back and powered it forward as hard as he could. The blow made contact with the curtain, followed by Ruben's face. The hand let go of his wrist and the rifle went light in his grip through the curtain. A split second later, Smudge heard Ruben's body slamming onto the wooden floor. Dropping the rifle, Smudge swept the curtain aside. Ruben lay on the floor struggling to get up. Blood poured from his nose as he looked around with glassy eyes from the knockout. Smudge stood over him, pointed his gun, and popped a bullet in the centre of his forehead.

'Hostile down, only Slade left,' he said, quietly walking away.

'Roger that,' said Danny, stepping off the staircase onto

the rusty metal gangway that ran around the lighting rails and ropes and chains and old backgrounds that would have dropped to the stage in between scenes. It creaked as he put the weight on it, causing Danny to freeze to the spot. Somewhere over the far side a creak echoed out, followed by a quick burst of fire ripping through the hoisted-up countryside scene in front of him. The bullets sailed past his cheek, so close he could feel the energy and heat before they thudded into the wall behind.

'Aargh,' Danny screamed, stamping his feet down on the metal walkway with a boom.

Moving fast, he ran as quietly as he could along the walkway behind the countryside scene. When he got near the pillar at the far end, he fired four shots through the fabric in Slade's direction, then spun himself tight behind the pillar. The returning fire was instantaneous. Bullets ripped through the fabric and hit the back of the pillar, sending chips of brick and plaster flying past Danny on either side.

'You see him, Smudge?'

'Roger that,' said Smudge, seeing Slade's muzzle flash from below.

'Let him have it,' said Danny coldly.

Smudge unloaded a full magazine from the MP5 he'd picked up from Ruben, the bullets ricocheting off metal walkways and lighting poles. A couple of white-hot stage lights exploded in the gunfire, and Danny heard Slade running for cover. Using the noise and distraction, Danny moved out and headed along the walkway to the front of the stage. He rounded the raised scenery and caught sight of Slade limping on the far side, blood running down his leg, his arm hanging from a bullet wound in the shoulder. He spotted Danny and raised his gun, his face contorting in rage and hatred. Danny was already ahead of him, calm and in control. He locked his target down the gun sights and tapped two into centre mass and one in the forehead in rapid succession. Slade stopped in his tracks and fell slowly backwards, flipping over the railings and landing with a boom in the middle of the stage.

'Hostile down,' Danny said, looking down.

'Roger that,' came Smudge's reply.

Ade lay behind the old theatre set trembling. He'd been listening to all the gunfire and had pissed himself with fear. When Danny and Smudge pulled him out by the feet, he nearly pissed himself again.

'Shit, that's embarrassing,' said Smudge with a big grin.

'Right, sunshine, you and me are going to have a little chat,' said Danny, ripping the tape off Ade's mouth and pulling the rag out.

'Anything, I'll tell you anything you want to know, just don't kill me,' Ade said, almost crying.

'Good, that's the spirit. Now tell me where I can find Lars Silverman.'

CHAPTER 58

Lars and Jasper arrived back at the Beaufort Gardens house. Jasper got out first. His six-foot six-inch body kept straightening up and up until he towered over the car. Turning his head on his thick muscular neck, he checked up and down the road before walking round to open the kerbside passenger door. A trainered foot shot out, kicking him in the balls. He moaned slightly before bending down to shoot a fist into its occupant's face, knocking her out cold.

'A girl with spirit, I should have expected that,' said Lars, waiting for his driver, Henk, to come round the car and open the front passenger door for him.

He walked up the steps with Henk behind him, the front door opening before he reached it.

'Jasper, bring her into the dining room,' he said over his shoulder.

Taking a deep breath to shake off the kick, Jasper took a cautious look up and down the street for prying eyes. When he didn't see any, he reached into the car and grabbed the woman's arms. He dragged her up over his shoulder and carried her into the house, still wearing the gym kit they'd snatched her off the street in. Moving into the dining room, Jasper laid her on a grey chaise longue in the corner.

'Keep an eye on her, Jacob,' he said to the man who'd opened the door for them.

Leaving them, he went to join Lars in the kitchen.

'How are the family jewels, my friend?' said Lars with a rare smile of amusement.

'They're fine,' huffed Jasper, pulling his buzzing phone out of his pocket.

He looked at the message, then at Lars. 'Slade has taken care of Pearson and his friends. They are on their way back.'

'Very good, excellent. This is turning out to be a very good day,' said Lars, frothing the milk on the side of his expensive coffee maker.

'What shall I do with the woman now we don't need her?'

'Kill her, but not here. Wait until after dark and take her somewhere quiet. Take Felix with you.'

'Ok boss. Thanks,' Jasper said as Lars handed the big man a coffee.

Parking the blue van several houses short of number twenty-three, Danny and Smudge sat motionless, assessing the building's exterior. Moving up in the back, Fergus stared at a satellite picture of the building on Google Earth. After taking Slade's BMW from the theatre, Chaz followed Danny and parked it a little further back from the van and out of sight of Lar's house. He got out and jogged to the back of the van, opened the door and climbed in.

'There's no way in or out at the back; all enclosed gardens. It's gotta be the front,' said Fergus.

'How do you want to do this?' said Chaz, the entire group falling back into their old team mentality with Danny as team leader.

'I'd like to rappel down the front off a helicopter and go in through the windows, but I think that option's out,' said Danny with a smile

'Yeah, remember the embassy in Kabul?' said Fergus, chuckling.

'Jesus, this can't be any worse than that,' said Smudge.

'If I give you and Ferg a leg up by the pillars of number twenty-one, you should be able to reach the balcony railings and pull yourselves up, yeah?'

'Yeah, looks ok,' said Fergus.

'If you work your way along the balcony and go in the first-floor windows, me and Chaz will storm the front. Standard sweep, kill on sight,' said Danny, leaning forward to look up at the balcony.

'Roger that, in and out before they know what's hit them,' said Chaz, sliding the magazine out of his Glock to put a fully loaded one in.

'Are you up for this, Ferg?' Danny said, turning to the back and looking at Fergus's blood-stained jacket sleeve.

'Try stopping me. I've got a bruise the size of a football on my back and some shotgun pellets in the arm. It stings like a bastard but I'm good to go.'

'Right, let's get on with it then.'

CHAPTER 59

They waited for a taxi to leave and a woman dressed top to toe in designer labels to walk her Chihuahua past them and around the corner.

'Ok, go,' said Danny, peeling out of the driver's seat.

They exited the van. Danny went ahead, turning and flattening his back against one of the pillars that framed the steps up to number twenty-one's front door and held up the porch and balcony. He cupped his hands together tight. Smudge stepped into them and stretched up as Danny pushed him. Grabbing the balcony's black painted iron railings, Smudge pulled himself up and over. Reaching back, he caught Fergus's uninjured arm and pulled him up as Danny pushed from below.

'You gotta stop eating the doughnuts, Ferg,' said Danny, moving slowly along the railings towards number twenty-three. With his handgun down by his side he gazed over at the steps leading down to the basement window and door in case any neighbours were looking out. Thankfully, most of the houses in this exclusive cul-de-sac were second homes. Owned by rich overseas millionaires, they spent most of their time empty. The last thing the team needed was a call to the police and a tactical response unit charging in before they got through the door.

'You ain't so slim yourself,' said Fergus, as he and Smudge mirrored Danny's movements on the balcony above.

Stopping short of Lars' house, Danny peeped his head down to check nobody was looking up from the basement. The window had been bricked up, and the heavy door to its left was windowless.

'I'm in place. You ready, Ferg, Smudge?'

'Hold tight,' said Fergus. He moved over the railing to the balcony on Lars' house and flattened himself against the wall next to the bedroom window. With a quick flick of the head to check the bedroom was empty, he waved Smudge on.

Rushing past Fergus, Smudge flattened himself against the next piece of wall between the windows.

'Ready to go,' he said over his throat mic.

'Roger that. Chaz, you're up,' said Danny.

'Roger that,' said Chaz, sitting in Slade's BMW.

He drove it past Lars' house to the end of the cul-de-sac and turned it round so the driver's door was on the opposite side to the house. Driving it back, Chaz stopped it outside the front door. Leaving it running, Chaz opened the drivers door just enough to slide out and crouched himself behind the rear of the vehicle.

'In position,' he said.

'Roger that. On my mark,' said Danny, as all of them tensed, guns out and ready.

'They're back,' said Henk, looking out the lounge window at Slade's BMW, its privacy glass obstructing any view of the passengers inside.

'Go, let them in,' said Jasper, rising from his seat to find Lars and tell him of their arrival.

Walking into the hall, Henk turned to Felix who was sitting on a chair in the hall, bored with his sentry duty.

'Hey, wake up, Felix, they're back,' he said, sliding a big deadbolt and chain off the solid front door.

Wandering through to the dining room, Jasper turned to Jacob and the woman he was keeping an eye on. With her hands tied behind her back and her mouth taped, she looked back at him with angry, burning, emerald eyes.

'Where's the boss?' he said, unimpressed by her look of defiance.

'In his office,' Jacob replied.

Turning away without answering, Jasper glanced out the window on his way out.

Why haven't they got out of the car?

His heart jumped as the realisation that trouble was on its way kick-started Jasper into action.

'Henk, don't open the door!'

Henk had already clicked the latch and the door was already swinging open.

'Go, go, go,' said Danny exploding forward, charging up the steps.

Chaz was at his back as he popped a bullet in Henk's forehead and kicked the door wide open. The sound of breaking glass tinkled overhead as Fergus and Smudge stormed the first floor. Knowing what Chaz would do, Danny peeled left and ducked his head into the lounge for a lightning look. Behind him, three pings echoed out as Chaz took out Felix with two in the chest and one in the head.

'Bedroom's clear, continuing sweep,' came Fergus's voice, followed by him and Smudge appearing on the landing above before moving off to the rooms on the other side.

'Roger that,' said Danny.

Seeing the lounge was clear, Danny turned back to see Chaz with his back against the wall and one hand across on the handle of the dining room door. Danny peeled to the other side. They looked at each other and nodded. Chaz flicked the handle down and pushed the door open. Before he could duck his head in for a look, a hail of automatic fire blasted through the opening, ripping chunks out of the stair banisters and wall behind them.

CHAPTER 60

Up in his office on the first floor, Lars jumped at the sound of fire. He got up and eased the door open a crack, darting back when he caught a glimpse of Smudge crossing the landing to the other bedrooms. Gently closing the door, Lars slid his hand into the bookcase and pressed the latch to unlock a secret door to a small staircase running down the back of the house. Sliding in, he pulled the door shut behind him and headed up to his bedroom. Cautiously pushing the panel open, he entered and ran across to his dressing room with its wardrobes full of suits and designer clothes lining every wall. He opened the nearest one and slid all the clothes to one side. Pushing the panel at the back, he forced it to one side, revealing a compartment with two Beretta pistols. Shoving one pistol in his waistband, he headed back to the secret staircase.

'Fuck this, keep him occupied here, Chaz. I'm going to see if I can get in behind him through the kitchen,' said Danny after the second volley from Jasper's semi-automatic rifle.

'Gotcha,' said Chaz, reaching round and blindly popping off a couple of shots to keep Jasper busy.

'First floor clear, we're going up,' came Smudge's voice over the earpiece.

'Roger that,' said Danny, darting his head round the kitchen door. *All clear.*

Moving inside the large kitchen, Danny went round the marble-topped island towards the outer wall, past the window and sink. It gave him a better view of the doors to the dining room on the far side. A movement in the corner of his eye caught his attention, Danny dived to the floor behind the island on instinct, dropping his gun as he landed. The blast from Jacob's pump-action shotgun destroyed a vase of flowers and a cake stand on the marble worktop above him, showering Danny with glass and water and porcelain.

Jacob moved out from the side of the big stainless steel larder fridge. He ducked from one side of the kitchen island to the other, looking for a clear shot at Danny. Shaking the debris out of his hair, Danny took a peep out from the side of the island, ducking back in just in time to avoid another shotgun blast. The cupboard door behind him imploded in a cloud of shiny veneered wooden chips, exposing a stack of pans and woks. Grabbing the wok and a cast iron griddle pan, Danny stood with the thick metal pan in front of him like a centurion's shield. He braced as Jacob fired, the impact nearly knocking him off his feet. Lowering the wok, Danny hurtled his other arm forward with all his might, releasing the heavy cast iron griddle pan at Jacob like a baseball pitcher. The pan struck end on between Jacob's eyes with a loud thwack. He went down, dropping the shotgun as he clutched his head.

Shaking the tears out of his eyes, Jacob scrabbled for his gun. Danny leaped onto the island and ran across its marble top, diving off the other end on top of him. Gripping his arm, Danny smashed Jacob's hand down on the tiled floor, sending the shotgun sliding away as he punched Jacob in the face. Drawing back for another blow, Danny saw a flash of steel as Jacob pulled a hunting knife from its sheath and jabbed it at Danny's side. It dug in but couldn't penetrate through his Kevlar vest under his jacket. Rolling off him, Danny grabbed the cast iron griddle pan and whipped it round, catching Jacob on his temple and knocking his head to one side at a peculiar angle. Moving the attack up a gear, Danny pushed Jacob back down and powered the heavy pan into his head over and over until he heard the loud crack of his skull caving in. Breathing heavily, Danny dropped the blood-speckled pan and got off the body. He picked up his gun and tucked it in its shoulder holster, then picked up Jacob's pump-action shotgun and moved towards the door to the dining room.

CHAPTER 61

'Hostiles down. House clear. No Silverman. Over,' said Fergus, heading back down the stairs with Smudge covering his back.

'Roger that,' came Chaz's response.

'Let's check out that master bedroom again,' said Fergus, sweeping into the big room to one side, covering it as Smudge came in past him.

They established the room was empty, relaxed formation, and started searching around while the sound of automatic fire echoed up the stairwell from below. Smudge worked his way around the dressing room wardrobes, opening them one at a time and brushing the clothes aside for a quick look. He soon discovered the one with the panel hanging loose at the back. Pulling it to one side he saw the compartment, empty apart from two boxes of ammunition.

'He's here somewhere and armed,' said Smudge, poking his head back out into the bedroom.

'Yeah, but where the fuck is he?' replied Fergus, leaning against the wall panelling as he bent down to look under the bed.

As he straightened up and moved away, the panel popped forward, causing both men to snap their guns up in its direction. Moving silently to the side, Fergus eased it open until it was far enough to see in.

'Fuck me, it's a hidden bloody staircase.'

'Danny, Chaz, we've found a hidden staircase, rear of the house, going down from the master bedroom. Silverman is armed, possibly hiding somewhere below us. We're going to follow it down, see if we can flush him out,' said Smudge, following Fergus into the small stairwell.

'Roger that,' said Chaz.

'Roger that,' said Danny, whispering on one side of the dining room door. 'Give me covering fire, I'm going in on three.'

'Roger that,' said Chaz, sliding a new magazine into his gun.

'One. Two.'

Chaz poked his gun around the door frame and let off a few rounds.

'Three,' said Danny, swinging rapidly around the door, already locked onto Jasper's large bulk kneeling behind a heavy oak table he'd turned on its side as cover.

'Fu—' Jasper started to say, as he turned his head to see his own fate.

The bullet from Danny's gun ended him abruptly as it ripped through his skull and he slumped forward.

'Target dow—' Danny said, tailing off when his eyes fell on Alice's shaking head, her eyes screaming out at him, her mouth still taped up.

Lars stood behind her, tucked in tight with only an eye visible from the front, his arm around her neck and the barrel of his Beretta against her temple. He backed her through the opening into the stairwell, pulling the panel shut behind him.

Danny looked over to see Chaz looking at the panel in disbelief.

'Smudge, Ferg, where are you guys? Lars has Alice. I repeat, Lars has Alice. He's somewhere in the stairwell on the ground floor,' Danny said, running to the panel.

He pushed it, then shoulder-barged it, but it was locked tight. The muffled sound of shots from within forced him and Chaz to peel to either side.

'Contact. He's headed down to the basement,' said Fergus, working his way down the stairs but keeping far enough back around the bend that Lars couldn't get a clear shot at him.

'On our way, don't lose him, Ferg,' said Danny, running for the hall with Chaz in hot pursuit.

Fergus came down the stairs so fast he nearly fell out the hidden door into the pool room. Holding back, he looked inside to see Lars at the far end of the basement by a heavy door. With his arm still around Alice's neck, holding her in front of him, Lars pushed the door open. A view of the steps up from the cellar and Beaufort Gardens was visible through the opening. Pulling Alice through, Lars slammed the door shut. Fergus and Smudge sprang out and ran to it, but the heavy door was locked tight.

'Lars is heading out the front with Alice,' shouted Smudge, standing back to fire shots into the door lock.

Grabbing the banister to stop himself on the stairs to the basement, Danny charged back up and ran to the front door. Ripping it open, he saw Lars slamming the driver's door of the still-running BMW, Alice sat in the passenger seat looking at him with pleading eyes. Flooring the accelerator, the car tore off towards Brompton Road. Danny had his gun levelled at the back window but couldn't shoot in case he caught Alice. Lowering the gun, he looked around. Behind the trees and parking spaces, a motorbike courier stood by a neighbour's open door, the two of them staring in disbelief at the war zone opposite. Spotting the courier's bike ticking over by the kerb, Danny ran towards it, tucking his gun in its holster as he went. He jumped on the powerful Yamaha Sport Touring motorbike, kicking it into gear before screaming off after the BMW. Fergus, Smudge and Chaz made it out into the road just in time to see Danny disappearing around the corner.

'Let's go before we lose them,' said Chaz, running towards the van.

CHAPTER 62

Danny sped down the centre of Brompton Road, ignoring the shouts and horns as people protested at his helmetless, reckless riding. He swerved dangerously between two cars when a lorry threatened to crush him in a narrowing gap, and emerged on the kerbside. Winding back the throttle, he undertook the crawling traffic, standing up off the seat to catch a glimpse of Lars's BMW carving up traffic as he pushed his way onto Knightsbridge. Danny's heart stopped in his chest when the passenger door of a dark blue Rolls Royce swung open in front of him, two Louis Vuitton-adorned feet slid out on shapely legs. Locking his arms and braking as hard as he could, the rear wheel lifted off the ground until he stopped just short of the startled woman.

Ignoring the looks, Danny bounced up the kerb and rode through shrieking pedestrians as they scattered, before bumping back down the kerb and accelerating across the junction onto Knightsbridge. He was a couple of cars behind Lars and closing as they approached the underpass at Hyde Park Corner. Spotting Danny in his rear-view mirror, Lars swerved hard to the left, just missing the start of the underpass wall, and snaked up the bus lane towards the entrance to Hyde Park. Danny had to throw the bike to one side, scraping his knee on the tarmac as he veered across the road going underground and the bus lane going up.

The traffic was bumper-to-bumper at the top of Piccadilly, leaving Lars only one means of escape. He came out of the bus lane and rammed between two cars, peeling them apart as he passed through to the sound of screeching metal. He hit two pedestrians with a sickening thud as he moved along the walkway through the gardens past the Royal Artillery Memorial and through Wellington Arch, scraping the brickwork before sliding sideways back onto the road. Weaving through the chaos in his wake, Danny followed a couple of car lengths away as Lars headed down Grosvenor Place, running parallel to the gardens at the rear of Buckingham Palace.

Watching in the rear-view mirror, Lars braked hard, trying to ram Danny into the back of him. Swerving wide, Danny crossed into the path of an oncoming car, passing it on the far side before swerving back to continue the chase. With his eyes still flicking to Danny in the mirror, Lars returned them to the road ahead. He tensed up in panic as a bus from Waterloo terminal pulled in front of him. Swerving hard, Lars accelerated in a desperate attempt to get out of the way, but the bus hit the rear of the car hard, sending the BMW spinning out of control into the corner of Victoria train station. Danny swerved violently the other way, ditching the bike as it slid from under him. It hit the back end of the bus with a metallic- and plastic-shattering thud while Danny slid and rolled past the back.

'You scream or shout, I'll kill you where you stand,' Lars said to Alice as he ripped off the tape from her mouth.

He jabbed his gun in her side while reaching into his pocket with the other hand. It emerged holding a metallic object which sprang up into a flick-knife blade before her eyes. Lars cut her hands free, reached across and pushed the passenger door open.

'Move,' he said, sliding across and climbing out close behind her.

'You two alright?' said a concerned commuter seeing the crash as he exited the station.

'Yes, thank you. It's nothing to worry yourself about,' said Lars, tucked behind Alice, his gun pushing into the base of her spine.

The man looked at them both, the scared look on Alice's face setting off alarm bells.

'I think you should stay there while I call the police,' he said, moving his phone to his ear.

Lars threw his arm up straight. The man's face barely had time to drop as he registered the gun in Lars's hand. Two loud gunshots echoed around the bus depot. Screams echoed a second later, and people ran on instinct as the man's body hit the ground. Lars used the distraction to move Alice into the busy train station.

The shots brought Danny's dazed mind back into the present. He rolled on his front and dragged himself up. Everything hurt like hell, but he seemed to be functioning ok with no broken bones evident. He focused his eyes on the chaos at the station: a crashed BMW, a dead guy on floor, people running either away from him or to his aid.

Where are they? There.

He glimpsed Lars and was relieved to see Alice as Lars

pushed her into the train station. Danny headed after them, ignoring the shouts from the bus driver behind him as he looked over the damaged bus.

CHAPTER 63

The station was busy, people lost in their own little worlds, spatially unaware and socially disconnected from the other commuters around them as they went about their business.

'Just keep walking,' said Lars, his arm around Alice's shoulder and his other hand prodding the gun in her side from inside his jacket.

They moved towards the platforms, looking up at the massive end-to-end departures and arrivals screens above the ticket gates. Pausing in the crowd, Lars looked around, searching the passengers until he saw what he was after.

He took his arm off Alice, giving her a reminding prod with the gun as he fished out a roll of notes from his pocket.

'Hey you, yes, you boys. I'll give you a hundred pounds for your tickets,' he said to a couple of schoolboys heading for their train home.

They looked at each other anxiously for a second before the thought of spending the money got the better of them and they handed over their tickets.

'Thanks, mister.'

Lars returned his arm around Alice's shoulder and guided her to the gate, tapping the tickets to open the barrier before moving her through. Looking along the platform, he spotted a train just about to leave. He didn't care where it was going as long as it was away from here.

In the middle of the concourse Danny stood completely still. His eyes narrowed as he scanned faces, clothes and hair colours, searching for Lars and Alice. He fought against the growing panic that he might have lost them. Lost Alice. Focusing on the task, two schoolboys excitedly waving fifty-pound notes at each other as they hurried to the ticket machine caught his attention.

'Hey, boys, where did you get the money from?' Danny said, his face as hard as granite and eyes cold as he looked at them.

'W—we haven't done anything wrong, mister. Some bloke and a woman gave us the money for our tickets,' said the boy, his bottom lip quivering.

Danny was off before the boy had finished, moving as fast as he could without breaking out into a full-blown sprint for the ticket gates. Weaving through the crowd, he hurdled the gate and ran onto the platforms with an attendant shouting after him. He didn't hear him; his attention was fixed on half a dozen trains with no idea which one Lars and Alice were on.

The hairs on the back of his neck stood up. He had the feeling Lars was close. Looking up between two trains, he glimpsed red hair, shielded from his view by the back of a man in a suit like Lars's. It was only for a split second as they entered the front of the train ten carriages away. The conductor blew the whistle for the train to leave, so Danny sprinted to the nearest carriage and hopped in the door just before it closed.

The train jolted slightly as it started to move out of the station. Danny started to work his way down the last carriage, heading for the sliding doors to the next carriage along.

'Danny, co— in. Can you hear u—' came Smudge's intermittent voice over his earpiece.

'Smudge, you're breaking up. Smudge,' said Danny as the train picked up speed.

'That's it, I can hear you now. We passed the bike and Lars's car. The police are all over them. Where are you, mate?' said Smudge, coming through clearly.

'On a train, I'm still in pursuit. Hang on,' Danny said, leaning over to a passenger. 'Excuse me, mate, where is this train going?'

'West Croydon via Crystal Palace,' the passenger said, giving a strange look at Danny's ripped, dirty jeans and jacket, and his hair sticking up all over the place.

'Thanks. Did you get that, Smudge?'

'Yep, we'll meet you at Crystal Palace. We're on our w—' said Smudge, losing the signal as the train moved them out of range.

Danny unzipped his jacket, slid his hand in, placing it firmly on the grip of the gun inside, and continued along the carriage. Sliding the partition doors open, he moved through one, then two, then more carriages, the thought of Alice quickening his pace as he got closer and closer to the end carriage.

When he got to the door to the last carriage, Danny stepped to one side, out of sight. He craned his neck and peeped in through the glass. There were only half a dozen people inside. At the far end, sitting facing away from him, Danny could see Lars's suited arm sticking out from the side of the high-backed seats. Sliding through the door and moving inside, Danny's hand tensed on the grip of his gun.

He got the briefest glimpse of Alice's red hair as it flashed across the gap between the seats. Forcing his breathing down, Danny focused on only one thing: putting a bullet into Lars Silverman's head. Halfway down the carriage, he passed the last passengers apart from Lars and Alice. With his back obstructing any view to the passengers behind him, Danny slid the silenced Glock 17 out of his jacket and pointed it head height at the back of Lars's seat.

He was within two seats when the woman laughed out loud, the mop of red hair swishing into view as she leaned across and kissed her boyfriend sitting next to her. The air left Danny's chest as he slumped down into the seat beside him. A rare feeling of hopelessness and failure mixed with dread and foreboding washed over him. When the train pulled in to Crystal Palace, he wandered out of the station and stood by the roadside, numb. Eventually Chaz drove the blue van up in front of him, the look on Danny's face silencing the barrage of questions they wanted to ask.

'I lost them. I lost Alice.'

CHAPTER 64

When they boarded the train at Victoria, Lars pushed Alice into the seats at the back of the empty carriage. He sat close to her, keeping the gun in her side at all times. As Alice looked out of the window, she saw Danny rushing to the train opposite. She wanted to scream, to shout, to pummel her fists on the window to get his attention, but Lars jabbed her with the gun as a warning. He smiled as he looked past her to see Danny enter the other train just as the doors closed and it moved slowly out of the station.

Still looking out of the window after Danny, Alice heard the click of Lars's flick-knife but barely had time to register it before he thrust it into the base of her skull, sending her world into permanent darkness. He sat her back as if asleep in the corner, got up and hopped out the carriage doors just before they closed for the train to leave. Straightening his suit jacket, Lars entered the station calm and composed, looking like all the other workers coming and going about their busy lives. Keeping well away from the police activity out the front of the station, Lars took a different exit, past the food courts and shops, to emerge on Buckingham Palace Road. After rubbing them free of prints, Lars discreetly slipped his guns and knife into a rubbish bin and hailed the first cab that came along.

'Where to, guv'nor?' the driver said with a thick London accent.

'City airport, and there's a fifty in it if you can get me there by four,' said Lars, pulling his wallet and passport out of his back pocket.

'Consider it done, squire,' said the driver, spinning the cab around to the beeps of horns as he cut up the approaching traffic.

CHAPTER 65

Two weeks later, Lars entered the kitchen and sat at the breakfast bar of his seventeenth-century house on the Keizersgracht, or Emperor's Canal, in the rich area of Amsterdam. His wife slid her arm around his shoulder as she placed a coffee cup in front of him and kissed him on the cheek.

'Daan, move yourself. School time,' Lars yelled.

'Coming, Papa,' came a shout, followed by footsteps running down the stairs.

The ten-year-old ran into the kitchen, happy and smiling. His mother came over to him with his coat and school bag.

'Come, Boris is waiting to take you,' she said, sliding his coat on and walking with him towards the door.

'Bye, Papa, love you,' Daan shouted over his shoulder.

'Be good, Daan, I'll see you tonight,' Lars shouted after him, his eyes never leaving the morning papers.

Mila Silverman walked Daan to the front door. One of Lars's men reached across and opened it for her.

'Morning, Mrs Silverman.'

'Thank you, Finn,' she said, ushering Daan out the door.

She watched him go down the steps and get into the waiting car. Boris closed the door and got in the driver's seat. Mila waved Daan off as the car pulled out of its space. A blue van pulled in to take it immediately afterwards.

Engrossed in the papers, Lars heard some metallic pops and traffic noise and realised the front door must be still open.

'Mila, Finn,' he called, relaxing a bit at the sound of the front door shutting.

He froze to the spot when three men armed with silenced Glock 17s, dressed in black with balaclavas over their heads, walked into the room. Two stopped just inside the door, their guns held by their sides. The one at the front had one hand on the back of Mila's neck as he guided her forward; the barrel of his gun held against her temple with the other hand.

'Wait, what is this?' Lars said, his hands up submissively.

The man sat Mila in a chair on the opposite side to Lars, then took a step back, his gun pointing at her head unwaveringly. Mila was trembling and tears started to roll down her cheeks. Lars stared with hate, the tension in the silence building every second.

'Look, I'm a powerful man, what do you want, money?'

The man still didn't speak. He grabbed the bottom of his balaclava with his gloved hand and pulled it up. Lars's face drained of colour at the sight of Danny standing in front of him.

'Don't kill me. I'll give you anything, money, whatever you want,' he stammered out in a panic.

'Whatever I want. I want you to suffer, the way Alice

did before you killed her,' Danny said in a low, gravelly growl.

Mila stopped shaking and stared at her husband, the reality of the man her husband really was breaking through the lie she chose to tell herself. Danny moved closer to Mila's head, his hand tensing as his finger put pressure on the trigger.

Seeing the revenge in Danny's face and the darkness of a man who'd lost everything in his eyes, Lars broke down.

'Please, please don't hurt her, I'll do anything but don't hurt my wife.'

The gun shook in Danny's hand as a tear trickled down his cheek.

'Danny. No, mate. This not you,' Fergus said, stepping towards him.

More seconds passed before Danny finally took a breath. He swung the gun away from Mila and put a bullet between Lars's eyes. Danny turned and was walking out before Lars hit the ground. Fergus and Chaz turned and followed. They left the house with the sound of Mila's hysterical sobbing behind them and jumped in the waiting van. As soon as the doors shut, Smudge sped away, heading for the ferry port in an uneasy silence.

CHAPTER 66

A shiny black Range Rover Sport pulled up behind an identical car outside Danny's house.

'Thank you, Frank. Take a drive around the block, I won't be long,' Howard said to his driver.

'Yes sir,' Frank replied, moving quietly off as soon as Howard was out.

'Morning, Tom. Mr Pearson's location?'

'He's in the Co-op on the high street, one of the lads will message you when he's on his way back,' said Tom, walking ahead of Howard to Danny's front door.

He slid some picks out of his pocket and went to work on the Yale lock, clicking it open within thirty seconds.

'Thank you, Tom. Be a good chap and make yourself scarce while I have a word with Mr Pearson,' Howard said, stepping inside.

'Yes sir,' said Tom, pulling the door shut and heading back for the car.

Always liking the upper hand, Howard headed for the kitchen to make a cup of tea and await Danny's return.

When he entered, a Glock 17 pointed unwaveringly at his head by Danny as he sat at the kitchen table.

'You ever enter my house without ringing the doorbell again and I'll put a bullet in your head,' said Danny, his unshaven face as hard as granite and his eyes looking at Howard, cold and lifeless from dark, sleepless sockets.

'Cut the theatrics, old boy,' said Howard, unfazed as he walked over and clicked the kettle on. 'How about a nice cup of tea and a chat?'

Danny clinked the gun down heavily on the table and slumped back into his seat.

'You need to get better men. I spotted the one you sent to tail me the second I left the house,' said Danny, reaching for a whisky bottle and a glass on the kitchen worktop.

'You won't find any answers in there,' said Howard, putting a mug of tea down beside the bottle.

Danny poured himself a shot and swallowed it in one.

'Maybe I'm not looking for any answers.'

'You've been holed up in the house for weeks. Paul's worried, as are your brother and friends. It's time to start pulling yourself back together, Daniel,' said Howard, his voice neither harsh nor sympathetic, just factual.

'And you, are you worried about me?' said Danny, resuming his intense stare.

'Good God no, I couldn't care less if you blew your brains out. But if you do decide to have a shave and join the land of the living, I have a job for you,' said Howard, letting the words linger as he sipped his tea.

The two men sat in silence while Howard drank his tea and Danny unscrewed the top of the whisky bottle, deep in thought.

'Well, as nice as this is, I have people to see and places to go,' said Howard, getting up to leave.

Danny stopped just as he was about to pour himself

another whisky. He put the bottle back upright and screwed the lid back on.

'What kind of job?' he said, looking up at Howard.

'The usual kind, bad people doing very bad things,' said Howard, walking towards the hall.

'Tell me more,' growled Danny, stopping Howard in his tracks.

'Have a shave and get some sleep, Daniel, I'll be in touch,' said Howard over his shoulder, the front door shutting behind him seconds later.

Danny stared at the gun and the whisky bottle in front of him. After several minutes passed, he stamped his foot on the pedal bin and dropped the whisky bottle inside.

ABOUT THE AUTHOR

Stephen Taylor was born in 1968 in Walthamstow, London.

I've always had a love of action thriller books, Lee Child's Jack Reacher and Vince Flynn's Mitch Rapp and Tom Wood's Victor. I also love action movies, Die Hard, Daniel Craig's Bond and Jason Statham in The Transporter and don't get me started on Guy Richie's Lock Stock or Snatch. The harder and faster the action the better, with a bit of humour thrown in to move it along.

The Danny Pearson series can be read in any order. Fans of Lee Child's Jack Reacher or Vince Flynn's Mitch Rapp and Clive Cussler novels will find these book infinitely more fun. If you're expecting a Dan Brown or Ian Rankin you'll probably hate them.

Ingram Content Group UK Ltd.
Milton Keynes UK
UKHW041915100323
418367UK00004B/117